THE STEAM KNIGHT

JON DEL ARROZ

PART I
KNIGHT TRAINING

RISLANDIAN TIMELINE NOTES

The events in this story take place after For Steam And Country.

CHAPTER 1

Wooden swords *clanked* against each other.

It didn't create quite the exciting steel-on-steel clashing sound I'd imagined I'd be making when I'd first entered into the Knights of the Crystal Spire. That would be reserved for when I reached a journeyman rank, or so my instructors told me when I begged them for a real sword. It only redoubled my resolve. I intended to be the fastest apprentice to ever become a journeyman.

The Crystal Spire loomed above the training courtyard, casting a shadow across half of the cobblestone patio, obscuring my opponent, Tristan, in darkness. Horseless carriages *whirred* in the background, echoing through the city streets.

Tristan stepped forward into the light. He had red hair and freckles, with green eyes. Like me, he wore loose training garb of white tunic and brown pants. We would train with armor later. I hoped by the time I made it to master knight, some of King Malaky's court scientists would invent some new rendition of the armor with mechanical cooling, or perhaps even the ability to fly like the airship that brought me to Rislandia City.

Those thoughts distracted me for a brief second, one Tristan used to strike. He thrust his wooden sword at my side.

I was too quick for him. I lifted my arm and dodged to my right. Tristan overextended, his weight precarious on his forward foot. Reaching across my body with my free hand, I grabbed his wrist and tugged him off balance.

"Hey!" Tristan shouted. He stumbled.

I spun, whirling my sword around to smack his back. The blow would leave a welt, but we were encouraged to fight as if these battles were real.

Tristan stumbled to the side, dropping his sword. He winced.

"Match to James Gentry," said Cid, the master knight who watched the class. The other boys clapped, but with little enthusiasm.

They didn't like me. The scowls on their faces said as much. Even though I'd been an apprentice for four weeks, I hadn't made a friend. The other apprentices banded together into little groups, but none would include me. Worse, they taunted me. "Oh, I bet James is going to go cuddle up with one of the master knights instead of share quarters with the other lowly apprentices," I'd heard Tristan saying last evening, when I went to follow one of the knights to watch his sword training. I'd been given permission to stay up late to watch him practice. It wasn't a negative thing. This place created hardness in people I hadn't experienced in the countryside of Plainsroad Village. I missed my family and my friends.

My parents were gone now, I had to accept it, though I didn't like to think about their deaths, when our farm had been overrun by Wyranth soldiers. It was just another distraction, something to pry me from the focus I needed to get through these lonely days. Back home I'd also had a best friend, Zaira von Monocle. The first time I arrived in Rislandia City, she'd come with me. But ever since she went on her mission to rescue her father, she'd barely given me any consideration. She was always off gallivanting on her airship, just like she used to complain of her father doing. Apples don't fall far from the tree.

My heart stung, just thinking about her. It ripped any joy I received from my victory over Tristan right out of my chest.

I returned my sword to the rack beside Cid, who patted me on the back in congratulations. At least the older knights seemed to respect me. They had, ever since I'd gone on my first mission to follow Zaira and help her in case there was any trouble. Because I'd been friends with her, they thought I'd be a help. Bringing apprentices on dangerous missions into Wyranth territory was fairly unprecedented, though. The others whispered that I was being treated with special privilege.

The knights didn't help matters when they spoke of me. "Pure unrefined talent like I've never seen!" I'd overheard Cid saying one evening while he drank ale in the common mess. I wasn't the only one who'd overheard it. Another of the apprentices, Reginald, had it out for me ever since that day. It was maddening.

"We'll break for the day. Don't forget, you have copying and scribe work to be done," Cid said, pulling me back to reality and away from my moping thoughts.

"Aw, don't we have a new printing press to send missives with?" one of the other apprentices asked.

"You never know when you'll be out in the field and need to drop a message. Scribe work is one of the most important duties we can do as knights. The kingdom depends on us to swiftly deliver messages," Cid said. He clapped his hands together. "Dismissed."

Everyone went their separate ways. I glanced over to the palace, wondering what Princess Reina, the heir to Rislandia, was doing. Not like she'd have much time to see me again. Though she *was* the one who took enough interest to recommend me for knight training. I shook my head and walked back to my quarters.

Under the covered pathway to our dormitories, I could hear echoes of the other apprentices chatting amongst themselves. Tristan was one of the boys, and a stockier boy with brown hair, Reginald du Current, walked with him. Reginald was a noble from Highview City, a place in the foothills of the Oler Mountains at the very northeast corner of the kingdom.

"You were supposed to be the one to beat that spoiled brat," Reginald said.

I bit my tongue. Spoiled? I had to work in the fields for as long as I could remember, and this noble accused me of being spoiled? I clenched my fists. But no, I couldn't confront the other boy now. It was best to hang back and listen.

"I know. He tricked me. He doesn't fight fair," Tristan said.

"Next time, you don't fight fair either. Break his leg," Reginald said.

My eyes went wide. What could I do? If I told Cid or one of the other knights, I would be seen as a snitch. That was the last thing I needed for my reputation. It wouldn't be good to head into the dormitory, either. If the boys were this heated over me, I needed to stay away until they cooled down.

I spun around and headed toward the spire. The words hurt, but they were just words. Even if they tried to hurt me, I'd outperform them all. I had to. There was nowhere else for me to go.

CHAPTER 2

THE SMELL OF BEEF STEW PERMEATED THE MESS HALL. MY STOMACH grumbled after the hard day of combat training and the intense focus of copying parchments for the last several hours. The mess was large enough to fit about two hundred people, though fewer than a hundred currently occupied the tables. The knights totaled about four hundred in strength, though most of the journeymen or above were out on assignment. Rislandia couldn't spare a man in this war against the Wyranth, and the knights offered a crucial support role to the Grand Rislandian Army. Only a few remained to train the next generation of knights.

I stood in line and received my bowl of stew before turning to the tables. None of the other boys looked up at me. They didn't want me sitting with them. It'd been like this for more than eight weeks since I returned from the Wyranth Empire. I was tired of dealing with it. All I wanted to do was to work hard and become a knight, same as them. Why did they have to make it so awkward?

I couldn't help but sigh.

A couple of journeymen sat across from me. They wore pins of the angelic wings of the Crest of Malaky on their tunics. They talked amongst themselves and didn't acknowledge the lowly apprentice across from them.

I was doomed to be alone for the foreseeable future. All I could think to do was throw myself harder into my work and prove myself as a knight.

When we were all settled and chowing on our stew, another journeyman stood in front of the room. Ethan von Lantern. He was a little taller than I was, with blond hair and a bit more muscular of a build. He'd been training with the knights for more than two years, and rumor had it he was due to be promoted to a master knight soon. In the meantime, he'd been designated as head journeyman, which meant he directed some of the other journeymen in their chores and gave announcements at mealtime.

Ethan cleared his throat. "Hello, fellow knights!"

"Hello journeyman!" everyone shouted back. Everyone's attention was firmly on him now, and the energy in the room lifted to where most had smiles on their faces. It was amazing what a few rousing words could do, and Ethan delivered them with a passion and intensity I wasn't sure I could copy. One day, though, I would be like him.

"The High Knight has one message for you. In one week's time, we will be having a competition among the apprentices. The winner in this class will be paired with a journeyman on real missions for King Malaky. If you do well here, you may be bumped forward in line to be promoted to journeymen. The High Knight asks that you keep yourselves well-rested, well-fed, and focused, so you might perform at your best. Thank you."

The apprentices cheered, all too eager to get in on the action, myself included.

"I'm going to win this so I can be paired with Ethan," Tristan said from the table behind me.

"Only if I don't beat you first," Reginald said.

"As long as we don't let James Gentry win," Tristan said.

The boys at the table laughed.

I fought the urge to turn around and punch Tristan. Instead, I angrily funneled stew into my mouth. They were right to fear my victory. No matter the competition, I would be at the top of the running amongst the class. I would show them.

If I became a journeyman, none of what they said would matter anymore. Winning this competition became the most important thing in my life.

CHAPTER 3

Eᴛʜᴀɴ's ɪɴꜱᴛʀᴜᴄᴛɪᴏɴꜱ ᴡᴇʀᴇ ᴛᴏ ʀᴇꜱᴛ, ʙᴜᴛ I ꜱᴇᴛ ᴏᴜᴛ ᴛʜᴇ ɴᴇxᴛ ᴅᴀʏ preparing my body for endurance. Most of the other boys ignored long runs, but knights were always on the go. I figured it would be best to get my heart pumping.

I jogged into the main training courtyard and looked up at the giant spire. Legend had it, the first settlers of Rislandia built the spire so they could look upon the entire kingdom. They had fled the area that now comprised the Atrebla Kingdom and didn't want their enemies to blindside them. Now, the giant spire was a symbol of vigilance and standing tall in the face of adversity. It was a sobering reminder of what a knight had to defend.

With a sack of potatoes on my back for extra weight, I started my run up the two-thousand steps of the spire. It was easy at first, but after the first couple of flights, my back ached from the bouncing potatoes. My shoulders tightened to the point of pain. Sweat dripped down my face; there was a long way to go. I couldn't stop now.

Several knights came down the spire the opposite direction, wrapping up their days' work. Only the best knights had offices within the spire itself, an honor very few would ever receive. They greeted me, but I spared no time to stop and talk to them.

After about the three-hundredth stair, I lost track of my place in the tower. Windows adorned every floor. I could see myself moving higher and higher, though the end wasn't anywhere in sight. My clothes hung heavy on my body, drenched in sweat, and my lungs burned. Had I at least reached the halfway point? My ambition outweighed what my body could physically deliver.

No, I couldn't give up.

With a grunt, I pushed myself faster. If I started to slow, I would give up. But I had to make it. I'd prove myself the best, worthy of going on an assignment with a journeyman. They wanted someone who never gave up, who persevered against all odds, who would sacrifice their body in defense of Rislandia. I would be that apprentice.

I didn't care if my body ached. I'd show the other apprentices that everything I did was earned, not granted. I would succeed, and I would beat them. With every ounce of my strength, I kept pushing up the stairs until, finally, I reached the top.

The top of the spire had a stone floor supported by stone walls with big openings to look out over the city of Rislandia. I saw two other people there. One was a knight, Lou. He was dressed in a regular ruffled shirt and coat like any civilian, and with him was another man, dressed much the same, but with glasses.

The man in the glasses was talking. "We'll pass the information along to our infantrymen along the northern supply—"

"Marcus, someone's coming," Lou said, holding a hand up to gesture the other man to be silent.

They both paused and turned to me. I breathed heavily, trying to catch my breath.

"You told me no one would be up here," Marcus said.

"There isn't. Are you one of the apprentices?" Lou asked.

"Uh..."

I don't know why this worried me so much. Perhaps it was the way they looked at me, or perhaps it was the odd fact that two men were meeting in this secret place, talking about the war. Why would Lou be passing information to a civilian, and in secret? Something in me told me to run back down the spire's steps as fast as I could.

As much as my legs and back burned from so much running already, I trusted my instinct. Dropping my pack, and hearing it *thud* on the steps, I hurried away from the two men. Heavy footfalls pattered down the spiral after me, echoing through the stairwell. They were trying to catch up. I had to hurry.

Without the weight on my back, it felt much easier to run. Moving downward proved far easier than the upward climb. Though my legs ached, I found myself moving much faster than before, able to leap over two or three steps at a time. Still, the footsteps behind me came ever closer. I pushed myself even harder.

"Come back here," Lou said. He was right behind me.

I didn't turn to look, but I felt a hand grab at the back of my shirt. He didn't get hold of any fabric, and I was able to slip past him.

Lou stumbed from his failed attempt. I heard him crash. I still couldn't risk turning to see what had happened.

"Agh!" Lou's voice echoed down the stairwell.

"I'll come back for you," Marcus said.

I kept going. The levels seemed to blend together. How far had I gone down? The light from the gas lamps at the bottom of the steps shone, revealing the courtyard. I'd made it. But I would have to find somewhere to hide. There were plenty of corridors and rooms in the knights' barracks.

Without wasting any time, I ran across the courtyard for the barracks. They were the closest to King Malaky's palace, in case the king needed quick assistance. Most of the knights would either be out on missions or getting ready for bed. I traversed the courtyard and glanced over my shoulder to see Marcus coming up behind me.

Returning my attention forward, I hurried through the main archway into the barracks. There was a big open room before the hallway and sleeping quarters where all the knights had their own rooms. I kept going into the thinner hallway, adorned by a brown rug. My lungs burned more than my legs at this point, each breath more painful than the last.

No footsteps came behind me. I turned back to face the courtyard. Marcus was gone.

"Is something the matter?" a voice came from behind me.

I jumped at the voice, spooked. When I turned to see who was there, relief flooded through me. Master Knight Cid stood in the doorway.

"No," I huffed, gasping to try to catch my breath.

"You seem frightened."

"It's nothing, just doing some extra training for the competition." It wasn't a total lie, but it didn't feel great to say it, either. On the other hand, I didn't want to burden Cid with the fact I was frightened by a strange conversation I'd overheard between a knight and a civilian. Cid had done so much for me already, and I needed more time to think about what I'd just seen and heard.

Cid raised a brow. "Well, you probably shouldn't be training in the barracks. I'll leave you to it." He turned back to his quarters.

"I'll be out of here in a moment," I said, doubling over to try to get more air into my lungs. I had the feeling something was very wrong.

CHAPTER 4

IT RAINED THE NEXT DAY. I HAD TO PRACTICE MY SWORD DRILLS indoors. In one of the big open rooms, I set up a practice dummy and worked on my moves. I held my wooden sword in my hands, wishing they had given me a real one. But I had to work with the tools I had. I practiced my stance, adjusting my posture from the attack to the defensive. The moves seemed awkward to me, unnatural, even though they were designed to provide the best footing for quick adjustments in the heat of battle. Cid told us we would need to practice these until they became instinct. I trusted him. I would be there one day.

After several moves, I practiced a quick jab at the wooden target. My practice sword clanked against it. I swung my stick several more times at the target, losing myself in the work. All of my thoughts evaporated. No more worries about knights being traitors, no more thoughts of the other apprentices treating me like dirt, and no more thoughts of Zaira von Monocle. It was just me and my weapon. This was the freedom that knighthood offered.

The sound of clapping resonated behind me.

I turned, expecting one of the knights or one of the other apprentices. Instead, I saw the most beautiful sight I could have imagined. And that included the first time I laid eyes upon the spire from the airship that brought me here. To be fair, I'd seen her before. Golden curls draping down just below her shoulders, warm eyes that let you know she loved life and everything about it, a small frame beneath an intricate dress of many golden folds and cuts that flowed to the ground. Princess Reina, King Malaky's daughter and heir to Rislandia.

"Don't stop," she said, smiling brightly at me.

It was all I could do to not stop *breathing*. I clutched the practice sword for fear of dropping it. My jaw had dropped in the process, and I snapped my mouth shut.

Princess Reina glided across the room. How could someone possibly move with such grace? She canted her head at the practice target, inspecting it. I had no idea what she was thinking. "I've spoken with some of the knights. They say you have incredible aptitude."

"Th-thank you, your highness," I managed to say. My voice cracked, and my mouth went dry. What was wrong with me?

"It's good," she said, smiling back at me. "Though my father formally recommended you, your entry into this program was my doing, you may recall. I so enjoyed our conversation in the palace when you arrived. I don't get to talk to many commoners."

I cast my eyes aside. Was that an insult?

"Oh," she brought her hand to her lips. She then touched my chin, lifting it so I would meet her eyes. "I'm sorry, James. I didn't mean it like that at all."

Her fingertips were cool, but they wouldn't be for so long with the heat radiating from my face. I must have been as red as a tomato. It didn't seem to bother Reina, if she even noticed it. Her eyes twinkled as she slid her fingertips away from my face. Every fiber of my body wanted desperately for her to touch me again, but I wouldn't dare say something so improper to the princess.

Reina grimaced. "I killed the conversation, didn't I?"

"No, not at all."

Despite my words, silence hung in the air. Reina let out a soft laugh. "You can be honest with me. I need to learn to think before I speak. That's what my daddy always tells me. I hope I wasn't intruding too much. I only wanted to see how you were doing." Her bright smile, which could melt snow, returned to her face.

I swallowed, my throat and mouth already dry from nervousness. "I'm doing okay," I said.

She raised an eyebrow. "You don't sound very convincing."

"There's really not many problems."

"Many."

"Yeah."

"Which means there are some."

Judging from the tone of her voice, she wouldn't leave until I talked to her in earnest. I set my sword against the practice dummy and leaned against the wall. "The other apprentices hate me," I said. Those weren't the words I'd intended to come out of my mouth. I didn't want to complain to her of all people. If anything, I had to be grateful toward her about everything involving the knights.

But instead of judging me, her eyes held real concern. "What happened?"

Something about the way she looked made me open up to her. I told her about the little things. The way I would be left alone when eating. The other boys talking about me when they thought I couldn't hear. Their constant vowing that they would defeat me. It felt good to let it all out. I'd been holding it in since I'd started training with the knights.

When I finished, Reina furrowed her brow in consideration. "It sounds like the other boys are jealous of how fast you're learning how to be a knight. It's probably something to do with their being apprentices and frustrated with the work. I haven't heard the knights say anything but praises of you. Do you want me to see if I can pull some strings and get you promoted to journeyman?"

I shook my head adamantly. "No!"

Reina recoiled.

That came out wrong, as well. Could I say *anything* right in front of her? I took a deep breath to calm myself. "I mean, no, thank you. A lot of the problem I'm having is because I was ushered in here without a proper recruiter. They think I'm spoiled because I have the king, your father, on my side."

"That's preposterous. We barely know you."

"I know that, but it's hard to explain, 'No, I'm really not close to the king,' to the others. I tried saying it my first day here, and they thought I was just trying to brag about how great I was. Whatever I do, I can't win," I said, my shoulders drooping.

Reina nibbled on her bottom lip. "I see what you mean. I'm sure if you become a journeyman, it would solve things."

"I need to do it on my own, though. If I can win this skills competition to shadow one of them on missions, it would set me on the right path."

"Is that why you're training so hard?"

I nodded.

"Ah." Reina sidestepped toward the door, her skirt flowing behind her. "I'll leave you to it. I should get back, anyway, before my tutors start to wonder where I've gotten to. I don't want them to tell daddy I've been ignoring my studies. He's already so cranky these last few days."

"Why's that?"

"Something about the Wyranth finding out our troop movements." Reina shrugged. "I know I'm supposed to pay more attention in case something happens to him, but I don't want to think about war. All that bloodshed..."

"Is it something we have to worry about?" The Wyranth finding out our troop movements couldn't be good. I remembered all too well how easily they'd overwhelmed my home. It had been little over a month, but it felt like an eternity ago. I didn't want to remember, or to think about my mother and father trapped in our small country house while the Wyranth mowed it over with their war machines. Thinking about it wouldn't make them come back.

"I don't know. Commodore von Cravat seems to think we're making progress, but I'd still much rather daddy be in a better mood."

Thoughts of the prior evening popped into my head. Lou, the

knight in the tower, told the civilian, Marcus, something about infantrymen, didn't he? Could this be related?

"Your gears are turning in your head there," Reina said, tilting her head as she observed me. "It's cute when you get like that. But don't worry about it. Just keep training and doing well. You'll have your time for glory." She winked at me, and without waiting for another word, she gave me one last glance over her shoulder and left the room.

Without her presence, the room felt empty. My mind whirled with so many thoughts I could hardly focus. Sword exercises were a quick way to kill all of those thoughts. Exactly what I needed right now. Getting into position, I lunged at the practice dummy again.

CHAPTER 5

After dinner, I decided to take a walk. The rain had stopped, and the air was fresh. I had to be careful—puddles dotted the cobblestone streets, but the gas lamps provided enough light for me to avoid them for the most part.

The evening had gone as usual. At dinner, I'd sat at the table, quiet and alone. The other boys mocked me, but I pretended not to notice.

The talk with Reina changed my perspective on my troubles. So what if I was alone? I had my best friend captaining the only airship in the world, and I was associated with her. The princess took time out of her day to talk to me. The knights were teaching me to be one of them. I should have been happy. But something was still missing from my life. Even with my dreams coming true, it felt so hollow.

I grimaced as I thought about it. There wasn't anything I could do about that. Not while I was in such intensive training. I had to stay focused, a cut above the rest. Reina was right, making journeyman would be my only way out of this.

A figure hurried down the opposite side of the street. The man had a long dark coat on, hands in his pockets, looking ahead and ignoring everything around him.

I recognized his face when he passed under a gas lamp—Lou.

What was the knight doing walking so hurriedly? Maybe it wasn't so odd. *I* was taking a stroll, after all. But what were the odds I would find the knight acting suspiciously, right after the strange incident the previous evening? I remembered what Reina said about the Wyranth finding out Rislandian troop movements. Too many coincidences.

In a snap decision, I turned around and followed him. When road turned into a bend, I waited for Lou to get far enough around the corner where he wouldn't likely notice me following him.

Eventually, Lou came to one of Rislandia's many taverns. The capital city was a hub for all of Rislandia, and even to the Atrebla kingdom beyond. Traders came from all over the world to Rislandia City. On any given day, it teemed with people ready to shop and sell in the marketplaces. In the evenings, they had several places to choose from to relax and enjoy libations.

After Lou went inside the Dovetail Tavern, I moved forward to see what he was up to. The windows were frosted, not allowing for a good look. If I entered the tavern, Lou would likely spot me. I needed another way. I looked toward the roof and saw a little hatch on the A-frame. If I could make it up top, I could spy from above.

I lurked around the outside of the building, looking for a way up. The back windows and doors had molding around them. It would take every ounce of my strength, but it was possible to climb up to the roof. I had to hope the roof itself wouldn't be too slippery after the rain.

I moved to the frosted back window. If I couldn't see in, the patrons inside wouldn't be able to see out either, especially in the darkness. It took some time before the street around me cleared of other people, but once it did, I gripped the top of the molding, digging my fingers into the rough material. It scratched, but I had to do it. I picked one leg up, and then the other, climbing up the window. Once secure and balanced, I slid my way across the window's lower support beam. The move up to the door's top molding would be the hardest part.

The shingles on the roof were my target. I stretched my arms out, pawing at the slanted roof. My reach was shy by a good foot. There would be no way I could make it without jumping. For a long moment, I stared at the molding on the door and the roof. It would be difficult to make it up, but moving with precision was exactly what I was training for.

This would just be another exercise.

I held my breath, pushing off the window molding, and leaped. Both my hands gripped the roof, and I swung across to reach the top of the door. My left foot managed to catch the corner of the molding, but it was wet, just as I'd imagined. My foot slipped. I shifted my weight to push myself toward the roof and flung myself atop it.

The roof surface scratched my whole body through my clothes. It wasn't just coarse, it was sharp. My shirt tore in several places, which I'd have to explain to the knights next wash day. They provided us clothes and expected us to care for them.

My stomach stung. I'd have several scratches there, but I didn't have time to stop and think about my wounds. Who knew how long Lou would be in the tavern, or what I might be missing him saying already?

I scrambled up the roof, losing my footing a couple of times as I traversed to the top of the tavern and to the other side of the building. On the way down, my feet slid, and I had to carefully grip some of the shingles to not fall. When I reached the hatch, I almost lost my footing entirely. I slid downward, about to crash to the ground below. From this height it would break bones, at the very least. At the last moment, I reached out and grabbed the handle. My body flailed, but I managed to hold on.

Using all of my strength, I pulled myself back up, scrambling to keep my balance on the roof. I held still to catch my breath for a moment, and then pulled the hatch open just a couple of inches, so I could look inside without being noticed.

I could see the tavern down below. Wooden rafters separated me from the patrons. The place was full, dozens of people at tables and at the bars enjoying the evening. I'd been in a tavern with Da once, after a day in the market at Plainsroad Village. He let me try his beer, but I found it bitter. Why people drank it I couldn't imagine.

Glasses clanked together. The bartender popped a cork out of a bottle. Where was Lou? Scanning the room, I found him. He sat at a booth in the corner, along with Marcus. Meeting with the same man again? Something strange had to be going on with them.

I wasn't close enough to hear them, but I also didn't want to draw attention to myself. I waited until the chatter below became a dull roar, and hurried inside. Then, I closed the hatch behind me and kept my body close to a large beam running across the length of the building. I crawled slowly, trying to reach a place by Lou's table.

It took several minutes, but I finally managed to crawl to a spot above them.

"...not safe to meet in the tower anymore. I'm not sure why I thought it was a good idea to begin with," Lou said.

"It's no problem. What's important is the information you have." Marcus produced a small bag and tossed it onto the table. Metal clinked inside, and I saw something shiny protruding from the top of it.

Lou grabbed the bag and tucked it into his coat. "The airship is on its way down the western coast right now. The bulk of the Grand Rislandian Army is by Loveridge, trying to protect the city from invasion. They'll be there at least another three days."

Marcus grinned. "Good. I'll see to it you're taken care of when we control this land."

"I'm just hedging my bets. I'm not so sure you have the upper hand anymore, with a von Monocle flying an airship again."

Marcus laughed. "The girl? She's not the same as her father."

"No, but her father is back, as well."

The conversation fell quiet. I couldn't believe what I'd heard. Lou, knight of the Crystal Spire, was a traitor! I had to bring him in, somehow, and stop Marcus from giving the information to his people. But what could I do from up in the rafters?

Before I could consider my next move, something tickled my leg.

Instinctively, I swung my foot around, kicking behind me. I connected with something small and soft that let out a squeak. A rat. And I'd knocked it off the beam.

The creature squirmed as it fell, plopping directly onto Lou's table. The sudden appearance of the rat startled the knight, causing him to recoil and stand. "By Malaky, what—" Lou looked up to the rafters. He stared directly at me. "You!"

I scrambled to my knees. I had to get out of here, quickly. But where would I go? Should I drop to the floor and run out the front door? If I climbed back out onto the roof, he would get to me before I made it down. The first option seemed better and would put me in a place where there were a lot of witnesses.

Lou and Marcus gathered up their belongings. They appeared more interested in running than fighting, for which I was thankful.

I crawled a few feet across the beam, and then swung over the side, dropping down and dangling from the beam by my hands.

The rest of the crowd in the bar took notice of me, the volume of conversation in the room increasing with surprise.

It didn't distract me. Instead, I let myself drop from the beam. I landed feet first on the ground but stumbled into a couple of patrons at the bar.

They didn't prove to be the friendliest. One whirled around, swinging a fist at my face.

I ducked. The blow missed me and connected with the other man I'd stumbled into. That patron doused the first man with his drink, and a brawl ensued.

Other patrons joined in, and the tavern erupted into a big fight. Drunks swung fists and glasses. I tried to slink away but found myself caught in the middle of the mob. Some of the patrons appeared to relish in the fighting, laughing as they pushed and shoved. I bounced between two large men and turned to see where Lou and Marcus went.

They weren't at their table any longer.

I turned again, scanning the room, dense with people fighting. I couldn't spot them anywhere. Did they manage to sneak out? Before I could determine an answer to the question, a blow struck me hard across the cheek. I stumbled. My jaw erupted in pain. I brought my hand to my face to try to protect myself, but as I did, something crashed even harder against my head. The world spun, and I collapsed to the floor in darkness.

CHAPTER 6

I awoke in a strange bed with the worst headache I've ever had. Grumbling, I coaxed my eyes open until my surroundings came into focus. White sheets covered me, and something was wrapped around my skull. The room was small, not part of the dormitory where I lived with the other knights. Where was I? What happened?

"He's coming to," a feminine voice said. Footsteps pounded in the hallway outside. The sound pierced my skull.

A woman dressed in a white nurse's gown came through the door, followed by Cid, who had a grimace on his face. "You got yourself into trouble, hmm?"

The memories flooded back to me. I'd been in a tavern, spying on a conversation between Lou and Marcus. "A traitor," I said under my breath. Startled with the recollection, I sat up quickly. Blood rushed to my head, and the room spun.

"Oh my," the nurse said, propping a pillow behind my back. "Don't strain yourself. You suffered quite the blow to the head. You'll need to rest up."

I grimaced. Not only did the world spin, but my back and shoulders were very sore. I brought a hand to my left shoulder. "Ow."

"We also found your shoulder dislocated," the nurse said. "We had to pop it back in. Would you like a painkilling concoction?"

"Please," I said, clenching my teeth together to fight the pain.

The nurse stepped back from the bed and slipped past Cid.

When we were alone, Cid stepped forward, keeping his hands clasped in front of him. "What's this you say about a traitor?" he asked.

I told him the story of the prior incidents, leaving no detail out. My head pounded throughout the retelling, but he needed to know. There could be no delay in stopping them.

"I had a suspicion there was something amiss with Lou," Cid said, frowning. His brow wrinkled as he did, betraying his age. "He was such a promising knight. This is terrible news."

I didn't know what to say, so I remained silent.

Cid sighed. "You did good work, James, but I have to warn you, what you did was also foolish. You should have come to me when you suspected something amiss, instead of pursuing Lou alone. Your aptitude is incredible, but you are no match for a master knight. If Lou had been more inclined to fight than to flee, you could have put yourself in mortal danger."

I frowned. "I didn't think about that. I just wanted to protect our people."

"I know," Cid said, his eyes softening. "But you can't be quick to rush into action. Part of what you're gaining here is a team, more than a team, a fraternity. The knights are your brothers, James. You can rely on us."

My first instinct was to think *like you rely on Lou?* But I didn't voice it. Cid meant the best for me. I could see that in him. "Okay," I said.

"Good, then you can get some rest," Cid said.

"But I need to be training for the competition so I can—"

Before I could finish my thought, the nurse returned to the room. "You won't be entering any physical competitions for at least two weeks. No, you need to recover."

My heart sank. If I couldn't make it into the competition, I wouldn't be able to work directly with a journeyman. I'd be stuck and other apprentices would advance ahead of me. I'd never hear the end of it. I felt bad for thinking about my own problems when there was far worse going on. A spy. Cid hadn't told me what he was going to do. He'd only listened to the information I provided him.

"There will be other opportunities to prove yourself, James," Cid said. "You've already far exceeded everyone's expectations. Recover. Get healthy. With the way the Wyranth keep advancing, we might need you at full strength sooner, and in a much more real capacity."

"Yes, sir."

Cid nodded and departed, leaving the nurse with me. She handed me the concoction that looked like mud mixed with a grassy substance. "This is the painkiller," she said when I took the cup. "Bottoms up!"

CHAPTER 7

THE NEXT FEW DAYS WENT BY SO SLOWLY, I THOUGHT IT'D NEVER END.
For three days, they kept me in the infirmary proper, telling me I
couldn't get up. When I asked for something to do, they brought me
history books to study, as well as the knight code of chivalry. With
nothing else to do, I managed to read a good portion of the dry
material.

When they let me out, I was happy just to be able to walk around.

"No using your sword hand while your shoulder heals," the nurse
warned me.

It didn't hurt all that badly. I rotated my arm around several times.
It was a little stiff, but no worse for the wear. Cid told me in no uncertain terms that I shouldn't even think of violating the nurse's orders.

"Why?" I asked him.

"Trust me, she is no kind mistress," he said, shaking his head and
walking away.

I wasn't sure what that meant, but if Cid told me something, I
listened. At least I could exercise again. I went on a longer run than
usual, practiced my stances, all while the other boys prepared for
combative games and tests of skill that would be coming the following
day.

The day of the competition arrived and the knights ushered us all to the outskirts of the city, where the city's main stable master had an arena for horse competitions. There were some wooden grandstands constructed on either side of the facility where we could sit while waiting. My entire day would be comprised of waiting, and I didn't have any interest in seeing who won.

All I wanted was to be out there, showing off like the others. The day opened with races, the apprentices running laps around the dirt oval comprising the arena. They kicked up enough dust that it made several of us in the stands cough like we were inhaling smoke from a damaged aether fuel engine. Afterward, the knights brought forth a climbing wall to test agility, and then made the apprentices compete in throwing bean bags at a target of varying distances to show their dexterity. I would have been particularly good at that. I used to pelt Zair-bear with tomatoes in the fields back home. Those were simpler days when it was just my family and neighbors, friends in the case of Zair-bear and me, but the adults always made obnoxious comments on how we were destined to be married one day. I could hit her from a full twenty yards off. My aim was rather impressive.

Reginald did very well in the dexterity contest, winning that portion of the competition with his bean bag pelting the carpet from more than halfway across the arena. None of the other apprentices came close to hitting it.

Once the points for the three preliminary rounds were totaled, the top four were paired for single combat. If I'd been there, I would have been able to best all of them. Reginald made it to the top, followed by Tristan and two other boys, Lawrence Holdwood and Stephan Retpa. They were competent in their own rights and weren't quite as rude to me as Tristan and Reginald were, but they went along with the other boys more often than not. Part of me rooted for them over the others.

I'd hoped Reginald and Tristan would be paired in the first round to knock each other out, but Tristan was selected to face Stephan, and Reginald to face Lawrence.

The stands filled quickly as people from the city finished their day's work and came to see the action. Pretty soon, there wasn't an empty seat. Rislandians lined the sides of the arena, as well. Journeymen and commoners cleared all of the obstacles from the prior rounds. The sun started to set over the horizon, but there would be plenty of light left for the main event.

Cid stepped into the center of the arena, announcing the contestants. Tristan stood across from Stephan. Both boys had wooden swords in their hands, as well as small wooden shields strapped to their off-arms. I would have liked to have the event show off some of the knights' technology. I'd heard there was a new aether-powered rotary gun that allowed thirty bullets to fire in automatic, rapid succession. However, it made sense why they wouldn't have the contestants shooting each other. There were rumors of some of the elite knights having bullet-repelling armor on their missions, but I hadn't seen it.

The match began. Tristan and Stephan circled each other. They took their time assessing, both too afraid to make the first move in case of overextending. That's where I had an advantage over them. I didn't mind making the first move. Sometimes doing so would force your opponent off guard. It worked on Tristan every time. I wanted to shout advice to Stephan, but it wouldn't have been appropriate.

Eventually, Tristan broke the stalemate. He swiped his sword with terrible form. I'd spent hours practicing how to swing elegantly, as if the sword were an extension of my arm, and it frustrated me to watch the others. I wanted to teach them everything I'd learned by following Cid's instructions. But even if I could, they wouldn't listen to me.

Moving first proved to be a good decision. Stephan tripped over the dirt while trying to defend from the blow. He fell to his rear, giving Tristan an opening to press his sword into his gut.

"Match, Tristan!" Cid called from the side, holding an arm up in the air.

Despite the fight being underwhelming, the crowd cheered. I didn't clap and remained seated. Tristan didn't deserve the win. It was Stephan's loss. There was nothing to celebrate. Both boys were moved to the side while Reginald and Lawrence took their places.

Cid made sure everyone was set and signaled the match to begin.

This match started off far more aggressively than the last. Both boys hacked at each other, blocking with their shields or parrying each blow. They came at each other with relentless fervor, but neither managed to land a blow. Lawrence pushed forward with his shield, which caused Reginald to stumble in the dirt. Dust flew around them, and it became difficult to see through the haze.

Reginald lunged and thrust his sword forward. Lawrence dodged, using his shield to knock Reginald's sword arm to the side, which gave him an opening to swing. In an amazing move, Reginald ducked. The crowd gasped as he managed not to get hit and throw Lawrence off balance in the process. It didn't last long enough for Reginald to be able to deliver a strike of his own. He had to retreat until he was safely out of Lawrence's reverse swing.

Both boys sized each other up once more, the dust settling so I could get a clearer view.

They charged, and more dirt kicked into the air. This time, the crowd around me stood, as if a different vantage could change what was happening. The people in front of me blocked my view.

And then I heard a boy screaming.

I rushed to my feet so I could see what happened. Lawrence was on the ground, clutching his leg. Reginald lingered to the side, a serious expression on his face.

Cid hurried forward. "Nurse! We need a nurse!" Others came in from the edge of the arena. One of them I recognized as the nurse who had attended to me. Everyone was too concerned with Lawrence, who cried in pain. He rocked back and forth on the ground, keeping his leg firmly to his chest with his hands.

"I think it's broken," someone said.

Those words made my eyes go wide. Reginald had threatened to break *my* leg when I defeated Tristan in a practice bout. Could he have...? No, it wasn't possible. I had to be imagining conspiracies after what I'd seen with Lou. But it was still too convenient. I frowned and seated myself while everyone remained standing. Should I tell Cid? No, if he saw foul play, he would have done something about it.

The crowd settled back into their seats as some of the people on the arena grounds brought forth a stretcher. They carefully lifted Lawrence onto it and carried him from the field. My two hopes at Reginald or Tristan being defeated were gone. Did I even care to watch the final match?

I stared at the grounds for a long moment while Cid and the others restored order to the field. Tristan and Reginald moved to their respective positions. No, I didn't care to watch and see who won. Neither of them deserved it. Tristan didn't have the control or the form, and Reginald didn't have the attitude or chivalry to be worthy of the honor of working directly with a journeyman. It should have been me out there.

But it wasn't. Cid moved to the center of the arena and proclaimed the match beginning.

I stood, slipping past others watching the display, and headed away from the event. More people were making their way toward the arena to see the final contest. Wooden swords clashed behind me, but I didn't look back.

CHAPTER 8

I STUFFED MY HANDS INTO MY POCKETS AND QUICKENED MY PACE AWAY from the arena. The streets were fairly devoid of people, shops and houses quiet in the fading sunlight of the late afternoon. I moved toward the large spire looming in the distance.

After a couple of blocks, someone came my direction—the journeyman, Ethan von Lantern. At his hip was a sheathed sword. A master knight would also have had a pistol on the opposite hip. He wore a brown coat, which flowed to his ankles, and a very clean black shirt. A satchel dangled from his back, strapped across one shoulder. "Aren't you going the wrong way, Apprentice Gentry?"

I stopped before him and shrugged. "I don't much feel like watching the last match."

"Don't want to find out who's going to receive special training from one of the journeymen?"

"Not really," I said, my words coming out rushed.

Ethan paused, his eyes narrowing as he examined me. "Because you think it should be you receiving the honor."

"I didn't say that."

"No, but I can sense it. And you're probably right, at that. I've seen your work compared to the other apprentices."

Why was I so defensive? He hadn't accused me of anything. I was just irritated because I couldn't compete. Before I could figure out what to say to his compliment, I saw another figure moving past him in the distance. A glint of light caught the man's face as he looked both ways before crossing the street, the afternoon sunlight reflecting off his glasses. Glasses! My eyes widened in recognition. Marcus, the Wyranth spy. He was still in the city.

But what could I do? Ethan was still searching me for a response and stepping into my field of vision each time I tried to look past him. "Gentry?" he asked.

I stepped past him. "There's a traitor. No time to explain. I might need help. Follow me."

Not waiting for a reply, I took off running. Over the last few days, I'd had very little I could do in terms of physical exercise other than run, which kept me in good shape for this. Ethan's footsteps padded behind me on the cobblestone street. It would be good to have back up.

Marcus had already rounded the corner, but he didn't expect to be pursued. He proved easy to catch up with. At the last moment, he turned toward me. His eyes went wide, and he tried to bring his hands up to defend himself, but it was too late.

I tackled him to the ground, throwing all of my weight onto him. His body slammed against cobblestones. The fall didn't keep him subdued, however. He managed to roll to the side, which caught me off guard and gave him an opening to get away.

Before I could get back to my feet, Marcus had a knife in his hand. His eyes were bloodthirsty with rage. "You've interfered quite enough, young boy. Now it's time you pay for it."

He cocked his arm back and slashed his knife toward my throat. I winced, but the blow never came. Instead, steel clanged against steel. A shadow fell over me. I turned my head to look.

Ethan stood to my left, positioning himself between Marcus and me. Marcus scrambled to his feet and stumbled backward, but he was no match for the journeyman with his sword. Ethan circled his blade around the hilt of the man's knife, causing him to drop it. He pushed forward with perfect footwork, which I admired from my vantage on my knees. That's exactly what I practiced and aspired to be. My jaw dropped as I watched him threaten Marcus with his blade.

Marcus held up his hands in surrender, but Ethan didn't let up. He pressed his sword to Marcus' chest, directly where his heart would be. "Please," Marcus said. His glasses had fallen cockeyed across his face.

"Please?" Ethan laughed. "My apprentice friend says you're a traitor. You'll have to give a better reason than that as to why I shouldn't execute you on the spot."

I opened my mouth to protest, but promptly closed it again. While a master knight had the authority to act as both police and judge in civilian emergency cases, a journeyman like Ethan could not. He could make an arrest and bring this man before a master knight, or to the civilian constable, but that was it. Even so, announcing the legalities didn't seem like a good idea at the time.

"What do you want?"

Ethan glanced to me. His eyes told me I needed to do the talking.

Placing my hand to the stone street, I pushed myself to my feet. "We want information," I said.

Marcus gave me a nervous smile. "I deal in information. Perhaps I can find what you seek. And you will let me go?"

"Sure," Ethan said. I wouldn't have been so quick to make a deal with this man, but if Ethan thought it was okay...

Marcus glanced between us. "What are you looking for?"

"You met with one of the knights multiple times. Lou. He escaped with you the other evening. Where is he?"

Marcus brought his hand to his head and ran his hand through his scraggly hair. "I really shouldn't divulge the locations of my friends. I—-Ow!"

Ethan dug the tip of the sword into Marcus' skin.

"Okay, okay!" Marcus said, taking a small step backward.

A cheer rose up from the direction of the arena. The fight must have ended, but I couldn't let it distract me. I kept my attention on Marcus. "Tell us," I said. "We're not messing around."

"I see that," Marcus said, frowning. "I gave Lou the location of a friendly house just north of Loveridge. It's halfway between the Rislandian Grand Army garrison and the town, set back about three hundred paces from the road between some trees. It looks abandoned from the road, boards falling, unpainted. You can't miss it."

Ethan nodded. "Apprentice James, I have some twine in my satchel. Grab it and bind his hands."

"You said you'd let me go!"

"If you found what I'm looking for," Ethan said. "I'm looking for a nice petite blonde girl with big brown eyes. Mm, mm." He grinned. "And you didn't help me find one of those at all.

His joke made me smile, and it made me think of Zair-bear. The description fit her perfectly, but something made me not mention that fact to Ethan. In fact, it raised a feeling inside of me that made me want to punch him. I wouldn't be so undisciplined, but I had to look away for a moment to calm myself down. He could find what he looked for elsewhere. Instead, I moved to his side and opened his satchel. Once I found the twine, I pulled it out, closed the bag, and paced around to the man with the glasses.

The man didn't resist. If he had, I'm certain Ethan would have made him pay for it. He placed his hands behind his back and allowed me to bind him. Once I was done, I stepped back to survey my work. "Now what?" I asked Ethan.

"Now we take him to the knights. I'll venture to guess they'll want to extract more information out of him," Ethan said. He motioned his sword. "Walk the path toward the spire."

The man was remarkably cool as he headed toward his impending doom, but then, this was a man who traded in spying and the secrets of kingdoms. He had to maintain an unreadable face. It was something I took note of. If I ever ended up captured by the enemy, I wanted to act the same.

CHAPTER 9

"You did well today, James. Between this and your actions on your unorthodox mission into Wyranth territory, you're starting to develop quite a track record. And I see you took my advice in getting help before engaging the enemy," Cid said, sitting behind his desk in his small office, which overlooked our training courtyard.

"Thank you, sir," I said, folding my hands in my lap so I wouldn't fidget. Despite not being in trouble, I couldn't help but feel pressure with Cid's intent gaze on me.

Ethan, seated to my right, patted me on the shoulder. "It was fun."

"Having the wherewithal to spot someone you've only seen in a limited capacity is impressive. It's part of why I want to meet with you today," Cid said. "You're aware of the program of an apprentice working directly with a journeyman on missions, yes?"

I slumped my shoulders. The last thing I wanted was a reminder of the program and how I'd missed out on it because of an injury. Worse, I'd heard Reginald won over Tristan, and though I didn't like Tristan much better, having a winner who didn't mind winning by injuring others didn't sit well with me. It seemed a wrong attitude for a knight.

There still wasn't enough evidence to bring Reginald's behavior to

Cid's attention. I didn't want to come off too smug or get a reputation for being a snitch. "Yes," I said, trying not to sound too bitter about it.

"Usually, we only allow one apprentice at a time into such a situation, so we can monitor and ensure proper care for when the apprentice is out in the field. However, in this situation, because of your aptitude, we've decided to make an exception." Cid leaned forward, a smile broadening on his face. "If you're willing, I'd like to further your education and have you work directly with Ethan von Lantern."

My eyes went wide, I turned to Ethan, who had a grin on his face. "Wow," I said. I couldn't have anticipated this at all. "I mean, yes. Yes, I accept."

"Good. I look forward to showing you the ropes," Ethan said.

"Ethan is one of our best," Cid said to me. "He came through the ranks quickly and is close to being named a master knight."

"I've watched him," I said. "I hope to become as good with a sword as he is."

Ethan laughed. "Well, thank you." A twinkle in his eye told me the compliment sat very well with him.

This was the best thing that ever happened to me, aside from having Princess Reina vouch for my good character to get me into the knights in the first place. It felt like I was dreaming. This would get me away from the other apprentices. Maybe once I was away for a while, they'd forget their jealousy and treat me like one of them. At least, I hoped. It could make things worse, but I didn't want to sour my proud moment. At the very least, it meant I'd get out of kitchen, or worse, *latrine* duty while I was away with Ethan. That couldn't come soon enough. "When do we start?"

Before Cid could speak, someone knocked hard on his open office door. "Did you tell him of his promotion yet?" a deep male voice said, one I recognized but couldn't quite place.

Cid stood immediately, so did Ethan. I turned, and if I thought my eyes went wide before, they must have popped out of my head now. I scrambled to my feet and bowed my head low.

King Malaky, in all his splendor, stood before of us. He didn't have his crown on, but even still, the king towered over all of us, his physique matching his authority. His eyes were dark brown, but kind, and he had a few wrinkles on his forehead, but it only served to make him appear all the more distinguished.

The first time I'd met him, it was as a civilian. Servants dressed us for a traditional audience with the king, placing both me and Zairbear in the most ridiculous of attires. I hadn't told her then, but she actually looked very pretty in her ruffled noble's clothes. We'd been so nervous that night. I still smiled to think of it. The hair of my arms still stood on edge with him around. Not that I was worried about him, but more like worried I would disappoint him.

"Please, no need for formalities. I came to your office," King Malaky said.

We all stood a little more easily after his words. He strode into the room. "James Gentry, full of surprises," he said with some amusement in his voice. "I could hardly expect that taking in a boy from the country would result in my receiving some of the best intelligence on the Wyranth we've had, well, since you arrived in the city in the first place. Perhaps the fabled luck of the von Monocles has worn off on you?"

"I hope so, your majesty," I said.

"I believe he's a bright boy with a good sense about him," Cid said.

King Malaky's eyes lingered on me for a long moment. "Perhaps he is, at that. Either way, the kingdom owes you a debt, and further one for outing a spy who was right under our noses."

"Who escaped," I said, wrinkling my nose.

"Which, incidentally, is why I wanted to talk to you three while you were assembled," King Malaky said. "General von Monocle has said his interrogation of the prisoner has confirmed the information he originally provided to you. We have the location where your traitor knight is in hiding and would like the situation dealt with."

He held a hand up to us to let us know he was still speaking and to hold our thoughts. "Tracking down and bringing in someone who's trained as a knight is very dangerous, but I know you would like to handle this within your ranks. And I also am aware of two capable young men who would be eager to undertake such an endeavor." He nodded in Ethan and my direction.

"It's too dangerous for them," Cid said.

"I agree, if they're alone, which is why I'll have them accompanied by two Grand Rislandian Army soldiers. Four should be enough to subdue a single man hiding in a broken-down residence. I'll also allow the allocation of an aether-powered rotary gun."

I clamped my mouth shut so I didn't yelp in excitement. Ethan's eyes lit up at the suggestion, as well. Apparently, advancing through the ranks didn't dull any of the excitement of handling unique weaponry.

"As you say, sire," Cid said.

"It's all we can spare at the moment, as we're having to retake the land down by Plainsroad Village. Most of our other personnel are allocated for rebuilding efforts where the Wyranth attacked." King Malaky placed a hand on my shoulder. "We'll be watching you, James. We're expecting a lot from you in the coming years."

"Thank you, your majesty."

King Malaky laughed and headed for the door.

Cid frowned, waiting to speak until the king's footsteps quieted as they disappeared down the hallway. "I don't like this much. Ethan, I'm sure you're ready for a mission, but not in the lead." He sighed. "That said, we are also at a premium for men right now, so I understand the king's decision. We'll support you like we would for any mission. You're going to have to walk the road, as we don't have any horses to spare. Rest up tonight, because tomorrow, you'll be traveling."

"That soon?" I asked. I hadn't even wielded a practice sword in several days. My arm was as out of shape as it had ever been.

"Ah, we need to get you a real sword for a mission like this," Cid said. "And you'll both need pistols, even if the king does provide you with this automatic gun. I'll make a list of supplies and have the younger apprentices pack them for you before you leave at dawn. But we can't have Lou out there any longer than is absolutely necessary.

He knows too much, and we wouldn't want any more information getting into enemy hands. Time is of the essence."

"Aye, sir," Ethan said.

"You're dismissed." Cid motioned for us to leave his office. "Oh, and boys," he said as we stood to leave. "Good luck."

CHAPTER 10

SOMETHING BOUNCED OFF MY FOREHEAD IN THE MIDDLE OF THE NIGHT. It didn't hurt, whatever had caused it. I was too groggy to think about what it could be, but I turned to my side on my cot, the bottom bunk of a bed. Our dormitory had four boys per room. Tristan, who had the top bunk of the opposite bed, snored. Albert and Lawrence, our other bunkmates, didn't' seem to lose sleep over it, but when something woke me up in the middle of the night, it meant I'd be wrecked for the entire evening. I had to fall asleep before Tristan or I'd never fall asleep through the noise. Another soft object hit me in the head again, making a light crinkling noise.

This time, I swatted at my face and connected. The hit made a slapping noise, and my cheek stung.

A giggle came from the doorway, a feminine tone.

I sat up in a hurry, spinning to see who was intruding upon our dormitory. A couple of crumpled-up pieces of paper rested on the floor by my bed. The objects that had hit me. I narrowed my eyes at a shadow in the doorway as my vision adjusted to the darkness. The woman was a figure I recognized. Princess Reina, with her long, flowing hair, dressed in a long nightgown.

"James," she whispered.

I slipped out of my bed and tiptoed over to her, trying not to make any noise as I walked. Tristan stifled a snore. I froze. If they woke up, I'd never hear the end of it.

Reina stepped aside to allow me into the hallway. Even though I was only in my nightclothes, some long-johns to keep me warm in the cool breeze of the northern city's evening, I didn't feel uncomfortable around Reina. I kept my eyes away from her. It was the gentlemanly thing to do.

We walked down the hallway in silence. Where could we go to talk? I lingered behind her to let her take the lead, and she wound me through some corridors back to a passage leading to the palace. It was a little strange. I recalled the first time she'd taken me aside in the evening to talk, when we'd first come here. I used the experience to tease Zair-bear, pretty much like I did everything else. She turned as red as a tomato. I smiled to myself at the memory.

Eventually, Reina and I arrived in a study with several wooden chairs with plush red cushions. Reina seated herself on one, and I took the one beside her.

"I heard you're going on a mission tomorrow," she said. Her eyes twinkled in the soft light of the hallway's gas lamps. The room was filled with shadows, but she seemed to brighten the room all on her own.

"Yeah," I said. Did she share everything with her father? It didn't bother me, as I thought about it. She was looking out for me. It was nice to have a princess doing that.

"I wanted to see you before you left. You know," she said, pushing a strand of hair back over her ear, "just in case."

I bit my lip. It wasn't a very happy thought, though the potential for danger was real. A sense of dread overcame me. I was going to be facing a master knight. It was amazing I'd survived the first two encounters with him. This was crazy. My heart began to race. But was it out of fear, or was it because of Reina's eyes fixating on me?

"Reina," I found myself saying her name. She had a very pretty name.

She scrunched her nose. "I said something that killed the conversation again, didn't I? I think I'm so used to getting things my way that I'm too straightforward. You'll be fine, James. My father is sending two great men with you and the journeyman. I believe in you."

Those words warmed my heart. My lips curled upward into a smile. "Thanks. I'm really excited. This is the first time I get to do real knight work, if you think about it."

Reina chuckled. "What about the time you went to the Wyranth capital to rescue General von Monocle?"

"That didn't count," I said, shrugging.

"Yeah?"

"Yeah," I said.

Silence lingered between us as we both looked at each other. What was I supposed to say here? Or do here? How, by Malaky, was I sitting here talking to the princess of all people, in our nightclothes, no less?

"I guess that'll be the way of it," Reina finally said. "You'll always be off on missions for the kingdom soon enough. I shouldn't worry."

"You...worry about me?"

"Of course, I do. I like you, James."

My throat constricted, and I found myself unable to speak. What did she mean by that? I was just a commoner. Surely she didn't mean it the way it sounded.

"Anyway, I know you need to sleep." Reina stood and crossed over to me.

I didn't want the night to end. I was perfectly content to talk to her, but I found myself standing, mere inches from her.

She reached out and took both of my hands in hers. "Stay safe and get that traitor, okay?"

"Okay," I promised.

Reina released my hands and hugged me. I stood there like an oaf for far too long before I finally settled my arms around her. I didn't squeeze her too tightly, part of me far too afraid of her touch. It felt so nice, something I didn't want to dwell on. What could I do about it?

She pulled back. "Goodnight, James." Her arms slid across my waist and back to her side.

I watched her as she glided down the hallway toward the center of the palace. I was thoroughly confused as to what had just happened.

CHAPTER 11

The next morning came all too soon. As I'd feared, I found it too difficult to sleep once I returned to my dormitory. Tristan snored the entire night, and my mind raced with far too many thoughts. Reina was among them, but I also had worry looming over me like a cloud. It wouldn't let my mind slow down.

Tired and irritated, I dressed and dragged my feet to the square. It would be a long day of walking. I'd have to trick my body into thinking I had more energy.

When I arrived, I found several people already standing there, including Ethan, the two Grand Rislandian Army soldiers, and Cid. The soldiers looked older than Ethan or me, one with a fully-grown beard, and the other having several days' worth of stubble. They wore gray uniforms with a pendant above their right breasts of the Crest of Malaky. Each man also had a matching cap atop their heads, adorned with a smaller, matching pendant. They had rifles strapped to their backs. A case lay at Cid's feet.

"Good morning, Apprentice Gentry," Ethan said.

I nodded to him and to the others. "Morning."

"I hope you had a good night's sleep," Cid said.

I shrugged.

"The packs are ready to go," Cid said. "I had a chat with the soldiers this morning. In battle, regular infantry typically defers to knights. Because this is somewhat of an unusual situation, that will still hold for the most part, but they are also instructed to act as guides to you, as these are both veterans in battle. Listen to them when in tense situations. Let me introduce you." He stepped to the one with the beard and motioned. "This is Sergeant Lansing." Then he motioned to the man without the beard. "And Lieutenant Fearson."

Both men muttered greetings to me.

Cid moved back toward the long case and bent to open it. Inside was a sheathed sword and two pistols, as well as another case for a longer rifle with a boxed end. It must have been the aether-powered rotary gun. "Your weapons are here," Cid said. He held up the sword and offered it to me.

I took the sword reverently. Part of my promotion to journeyman would be working with a blacksmith to forge my own blade. This would be a stand-in, but it was amazing enough to be able to hold real steel in my hands. It was heavy, but not so much to be a burden. I slid the sword into the scabbard at the side of my belt and fastened the clasp. It felt good there.

Cid then handed Ethan and me our pistols. We clasped them to the other sides of our belts. While we readied ourselves, Cid held the case with the rotary gun. "I'm going to have Ethan carry this with his pack. Ethan, you're in charge of it. With a device like this, you know not to let it fall into enemy hands. No matter what."

"Of course, sir," Ethan said. He stretched out his arms to take the weapon.

Cid wore a concerned expression on his face. His honesty superseded his ability to keep himself measured around us. While it might not have been the most advisable for troop morale, it made me realize he cared about us as more than just expendable units. We were family. His children, in a way.

"Very well. Stay safe on your mission. Remember all we taught you and do Rislandia proud," Cid said. His forehead and chin wrinkled as he grew more serious. "For steam and country."

"For steam and country!" we echoed.

With that, we grabbed our packs and strapped them to our backs, bid Cid farewell, and headed to the road.

CHAPTER 12

HOURS PASSED. THOUGH THE SCENERY OF RISLANDIA WAS NICE THIS time of year with its green grasses and hills along the countryside, it also became monotonous after so much time. Several small villages lay along the outskirts of Rislandia, but we had long since passed beyond those into open space. The only change to mark the passage of time was the sun moving from one end of the horizon to the other.

The soldiers talked amongst themselves. Ethan and I stuck together. Even though we were one team, there was a separation between us. Something that made us knights and them infantry. It didn't make any sense, but it was there, nonetheless.

Having started the day tired, my energy only dwindled by midday. Ethan suggested we take a break, for which I was grateful. I needed a nap more than anything else, but we had to keep going. There was a traitor out there, and we had to bring him to justice quickly.

I sat on my pack, content enough to get off my feet and have the weight off my shoulders. The others did the same, and we formed a circle. Ethan set his additional case beside him.

"Should we test it out?" I asked, motioning my head toward the rotary gun.

"We should probably save the ammunition," Ethan said.

"Gentry has a point," Lieutenant Fearson said. He chewed on some green substance and spit it to the side of him. "You'll want to know how it fires before taking it into combat. Lotta rifles got a kick, and you gotta be ready for it."

Ethan bent over toward the case and popped it open. He had a grin on his face which made me jealous to see him holding it. The gun looked much like any other from the barrel on back, though attached to the stock was a copper tube with a small compartment for the aether fuel. It held a small steam motor that turned gears inside the stock to fire the bullets in rapid succession.

I was lucky I didn't drool on it.

"Alright, let's try it," Ethan said. He picked up the gun and stood.

"Shoot the tree over there," Sergeant Lansing said, pointing to an oak about twenty yards out.

Ethan held the gun up to his shoulder and looked through the sights, his arms awkwardly avoiding the long magazine of bullets protruding from the bottom. He held his face a good distance from the gun, and it looked snug in his shoulder.

I recalled the first time I'd fired a rifle. My Da let me shoot his when I was eight years old. I had set my chin directly on the gun, and I paid for it. The stock kicked up hard and hit me in the jaw. I was lucky I didn't lose any teeth. I also never made that mistake again.

Ethan pulled the trigger and held it. The barrel lifted and kicked to the left as each bullet blasted from the chamber. *Tat-tat-tat-tat-tat.* The first couple of bullets hit the tree, but the others went astray. Ethan pulled the gun back to its proper aim after several more shots. Splinters of wood sprayed off of the thick tree trunk. After he'd fired about twenty bullets, Ethan stopped.

"Wow," he said. "That was crazy."

"A fine weapon. Dangerous," Lieutenant Fearson said, eyes narrowed at the target. "It looks like you hit the target with about two-thirds of the bullets. Now you'll know you have to keep it from pulling."

"It took about all my strength to keep it steady," Ethan said.

I held my arms out. "My turn."

Ethan grinned at me. "I don't think so."

My heart sank. All I wanted to do was fire that contraption. I was the one who'd urged him to try it out. My bottom lip jutted out, my natural response to pout, but I clamped my jaw shut so I would remain stoic. I was a man now, a knight, and I needed to act like one. "Come on, I should figure out how to use it, too."

"You won't be using this in a combat situation. As your mentor, it would be wrong of me to let an apprentice have such a privilege."

The two infantrymen looked amused at our interchange. But I couldn't argue with Ethan further. He was my superior, and I had to show I could be relied upon to obey in situations like this if I wanted to become a journeyman.

"Okay," I said. It still irritated me, but I did what I had to do. "We should get moving again if we want to make good time."

Ethan's eyes seemed to hold more respect for me. He nodded. "You heard the apprentice. He doesn't like to take too long of breaks. Let's get going!"

CHAPTER 13

As the sun set on the second day of our hike down the road from Rislandia City, we came close to our mark. We paused and moved off the road so our encampment wouldn't draw any attention from Lou or anyone working for him. Lieutenant Fearson assured us we were about an hour's walk from where we wanted to go, and our location would give plenty of space between us and them.

"He doesn't know where to look for us," Fearson said, "or possibly even that we're coming. He'll be on guard, but we'll be fine as long as one of us keeps watch. Best way to do it is to take shifts so everyone can get a solid amount of sleep. Each of us can take two hours." He reached into the vest of his uniform and produced a small pocket watch. "I even brought a way to keep time."

"Perfect," Ethan said. "Before that, we should probably scout what we're up against, since it's not too late. We'll leave our packs here and..." he glanced between us. "Ordinarily, I'd have James keep watch, but I think it'd be better to have someone who's had a little more gun training, in case of bandits. Sergeant Lansing, would you mind?"

The soldier nodded.

"Good. Set up whatever you need for camp, and we'll be back no later than three hours from now. If we're gone longer, go back to the closest garrison and tell them we're in trouble. Hopefully, they're not out on patrol or already engaged with the enemy." Ethan frowned. "Though, I guess King Malaky wouldn't have sent us if there were easy backup."

I shifted my weight. The thought was uncomfortable. But, hopefully, Lou wouldn't prove to be too much trouble. On the other hand, he was a master knight, which meant he'd performed far beyond what the rest of us had accomplished. I'd seen knights in action before when we had to rescue Baron von Monocle. They were incredible fighters. But surely four of us...

It would do no good to fret. I took a deep breath to calm myself. We had work to do, and we would do it.

The three of us took pistols, easy to carry and quick to maneuver. Ethan and I left our swords behind so they wouldn't move or clank against anything while we were trying to be stealthy. Our mission tonight was simple: get a lay of the land, see what we could, and prepare for an assault on our terms.

We walked down the main road, with Fearson leading the way.

"I've patrolled this road before, I'm pretty sure I know the place we're looking for," he said as we walked.

"You're doing really well," Ethan said to me, keeping his voice low, with shadows of night cast over his face.

"Thanks," I said.

"You could probably use more combat training, I'm sure. We'll work on some of that when we're done with this mission."

After that, we fell into silence. We wouldn't be able to talk much as we approached. Too much risk of being heard. I noticed the way Ethan's gait changed. He seemed to move more lightly on the balls of his feet. Each step made less noise as we traversed.

When we came close to Lou's location, Fearson slowed in his step and moved into in the short grass to the side of the road. It muted our footsteps completely. He motioned for us to follow, and we turned off the main road.

Just as Marcus had described, trees covered an area ahead. We moved toward them, crouching low and slowing our paces.

The frame of a two-story, box of a house lay just beyond the trees. I couldn't make out many of the details of it from this distance, but that's what we were here to determine.

The inside of the house was pure darkness. No lights trickled through the exterior. It looked dead, or at the very least, Lou was being cautious about hiding.

We pressed onward, making our way through the trees. Ethan grabbed me by the arm, and I stopped moving. He brought his face close to my ear and whispered, "You stay here and watch for anything strange. If you see someone coming or anything amiss, head back right away. Understand?"

I wanted to help him survey the house, but they needed someone to take point further back, and to get back to Lansing if worse came to worst. I nodded.

Ethan moved away from me then. He and Fearson split up and circled around the house in opposite directions. I watched from the trees, pressing against one of them to keep hidden. So far, there wasn't any sign of Lou or anyone else.

Several minutes passed while my companions circled their way around the house. My eyes began to adjust to the utter darkness. I saw where windows should have been. They were boarded up, with a couple loose pieces of wood dangling and revealing more darkness inside. The house looked rundown, weeds overgrown at its base. It made the hairs on my arms stand on edge.

A hand grabbed me by the wrist. The grip was strong, stinging me.

I jerked my arm back, managing to break his grip with the full weight of my body pulling away. In the darkness, I couldn't get a good look at my assailant, but it wasn't Ethan or Fearson. The man reached for me again with both of his massive arms. This time, I managed to duck. I lunged to his side to get past him, able to move faster than him. I took off running.

Despite Ethan's warning to stay quiet, I figured it would be best to warn my allies. "Someone's outside the house! He's coming after me!" I shouted.

I heard some scuffling behind me, but Ethan and Fearson didn't betray their positions. There was no time to look back and see if they were coming toward me. Heavy footsteps fell behind me. I darted into the woods.

Instead of going directly to the road, I weaved between the trees to try to throw off my attacker. I didn't know the terrain very well, but I could see the outlines of most of the foliage in the dark. I had to be careful to jump over some roots.

My gambit worked. The man behind me cursed, and I heard the *smack* of a body crashing into some bushes. He must have hit the root I'd just narrowly dodged.

I took off running at full speed. Soon, I passed the trees into the open area. There would be no hiding from this point forward. The landscape was too open. I had to run as hard as I could to put distance between me and the attacker. And I had to hope the others made it to safety.

It was a good thing I'd spent all of my down time running over these last weeks. It built my stamina, making a hard run over a long duration far easier than it would have been otherwise. My lungs cried for more air, but not like they would have if I hadn't been ready for it. My footsteps fell in a rapid rhythm as I rushed down the road.

CHAPTER 14

For nearly the full hour it took to return to our campsite, I didn't let up in my pace. Sweat dripped down my face, and even with my extended training, I found myself wearing down. It was late, and I'd exerted too much energy. Once my adrenaline wore off, I was ready for a good night's sleep. But would I be able to get one?

No one seemed to have followed me. I checked over my shoulder several times, finally slowing to a jog. If my enemy wasn't in sight after this far, odds were that I was safe. Farther down the road, I noted the surroundings to be where we had turned to make our camp.

When I arrived, Sergeant Lansing was fast asleep. The fire he'd set up between our packs had gone out. He used his pack as a pillow and looked rather peaceful.

"Lansing," I said, my voice in a half-whisper despite being in the open air.

He stirred, turning to the side before hurrying to sit up. "Huh? What?" He reached for his pistol, but realization of my identity crossed his face. He let his hand fall to his side. "Gentry, you scared me." His eyes went wide. "It's only you."

"Yeah, I ran into some trouble back at the house. We were discovered."

"How many were there?"

I shrugged. "Uncertain. I only saw one chasing me, but there could have been more inside."

"Hmm," Lansing said, frowning in thought. "I'm not sure what to do."

"Me either. I think we should probably wait an hour or so to see if they come back. Maybe they had to hide and were making their way back after me. I ran pretty hard."

"Yeah, good point."

I sat on my pack. We waited for the others. After a while, weariness overcame me, and my eyes became too heavy to keep open. Lansing didn't provide much company. He wasn't the type to talk much, and I could tell he was rattled by the prospect of losing Fearson. It made for an uncomfortable wait.

The wind picked up, blowing across the tall grasses of the plains. I gave into my weariness. Maybe I could rest my eyes for just a little while...

When I opened them again, I found myself falling off my pack. Lansing had drifted back asleep, which meant we were completely unguarded. The wind had died down, but the sound of footsteps in the grass drew my attention. Someone was coming toward us.

I scrambled to my feet, reaching for my pistol. I fumbled it, still unused to grabbing for a gun at my belt. A shadowy figure appeared in my peripheral vision. If it was someone wanting to attack us, I wouldn't have been able to get a shot off first.

In the process of my movements, Lansing stirred. He looked at me groggily and turned himself toward the figure.

Fortunately, as the figure came closer, I saw it was Ethan. His clothes were torn and dusty, and he looked none too happy to be there. "Easy there, Apprentice," Ethan said, putting his hands up. "Don't shoot your mentor."

"I wasn't going to," I said, letting my hand slide away from the hilt of my pistol. "You're okay. What about Fearson?"

Ethan shook his head, circling through the camp and plopping down on his pack. He let out a deep sigh. "I didn't meet up with him again. Once you shouted, I jumped into a ditch behind the house and kept cover there for a while. When I thought it was safe, I crawled away from the house until I was sure I was far enough away not to be seen."

"If you were crawling, then he should have been back by now, assuming he was on his feet the whole way."

"Yeah." Ethan frowned.

The three of us fell silent as we considered the possibilities of what happened to him. None of the scenarios I imagined could have gone well for Fearson. "So, what do we do?"

Ethan bit his lip. "We have to continue with the mission as planned. If Fearson was captured, we can rescue him. If not, there's nothing we can do. Now that I know the layout, I think we travel around the house to the back ditch, crawl from there. The house has a basement with a hatch in the back of it. We can sneak inside and take Lou by surprise."

"Is it just the one enemy?" Lansing asked.

Ethan shook his head. "I'm not certain. We know James encountered someone. Did it look like Lou?"

"I couldn't tell," I said.

"Too bad. Either way, it doesn't matter. There can't be more than a few of them, and they only have one knight." Ethan gazed back in the direction of the old house where Lou was hiding. "Here's the plan. We get some sleep. Hopefully, Fearson comes back by morning. If not, we handle the situation and bring Lou to justice."

He sounded so confident. Despite the very stressful evening, I found myself nodding in agreement and feeling much safer.

Wrinkles formed around Lansing's eyes as he considered. "We fight tomorrow."

"Okay, lie down and try to get some sleep. I'll keep first watch. James, you've got second, and Lansing third," Ethan said.

We muttered our agreements and unrolled the blankets from our packs. I lay down and closed my eyes, but despite my weariness, I found it very difficult to stop thinking and sleep. What if Lou was too much for us to handle? He'd spotted us in the dark. This mission wasn't going to be the quick, easy capture like I'd thought it was going to be. We were faced with a master knight, and that was something to fear.

CHAPTER 15

WHEN WE SET OUT THE NEXT DAY, WE DECIDED TO LEAVE OUR PACKS again. If we succeeded, we could come back and get them, or at the very worst, we could make our way to Loveridge and request the civilians there give us provisions before our journey back. Either way, we wouldn't need the extra weight on our backs. This time, we clipped our scabbards to our belts. Ethan brought the rotary gun, keeping the extra magazine of ammunition at his side. My jealousy flared anew, but I didn't say anything.

Sergeant Lansing remained quiet the entire morning while we prepared to break camp. He was closer with Fearson than we were, and I could only imagine what was going through his head. He kept to the task at hand, neatly piling all of his belongings before we departed.

The three of us walked in silence for a long time. We had nothing to say, no plans to go over. All we had to do was execute Ethan's plan. Thinking of the impending battle kept me from wanting conversation.

I'd been in worse situations before. This was at least in my own country, in an area where I felt somewhat comfortable. Traversing the hills into Wyranth territory had been some of the most frightening moments of my life. We travelled through that countryside, pretending to be civilians, but what if we'd been discovered?

Cid had kept me calm then, and though he wasn't here now, Ethan had a similar effect on me. Was that how knights were supposed to be? Like a cane or a hoe to hold you upright when you're working hard in summer days and need something to lean on.

We'd made it, but at the cost of Frances' life. I'd barely gotten to know him. I hoped I wouldn't have to lose one of my traveling companions here. The thought was so morbid I couldn't even look at the others for a while.

I shook my head, forcing myself to think of something else. What else did I have to look forward to? Seeing Reina again? Or Zair-bear? Another complicated mess. Why couldn't I just think about simple things like everyone else seemed to do?

It wasn't long before we found our way back to Lou's hideaway. The trees were easier to spot during the daylight. Part of the reason Ethan wanted to attack during daytime was that they wouldn't expect it, but they'd be waiting for us to return at night. Or so he explained to us back at the camp. It made sense to me. In the darkness, Lou would have an edge in knowledge of the area, and it made it more dangerous for us to pursue him.

We broke from the main road into the grasses, this time taking a wide berth around the house. We came to a small creek and followed it toward the house and the cluster of trees. The ditch lay ahead of us. The creek took a hard turn to our left, away from the house. Once we came close to the ditch, Ethan hurried to crouch down in it. We both followed.

The house was as dead as the prior evening. Ethan put a finger to his lips to remind us to be quiet. Then, we waited.

Wind wasn't so much of a factor during the day. In fact, the stagnating air caused me to sweat after so much exercise. I undid the top button of my shirt, though that didn't provide much relief. No one in the house stirred or seemed to notice us, if they were still there at all. In the daytime, it looked even more worn. Chipped brown paint appeared as old as I was. The roof shingles were in disarray, some having fallen off. No one had kept this place up in a long time. The basement entrance was right where Ethan said it would be. Would it be locked, though? Given the state of the rest of the house, if it had a lock, it might have been rotted.

After several minutes of waiting, Ethan slid the strap on the rotary gun so it clung to his back. He crawled on his belly toward the house. Lansing and I followed. I moved, limb over limb, across the rough dirt and grass, which scratched my stomach as I moved. I wouldn't complain, however. If this was the worst of the pain I'd have to take to serve Rislandia, then so be it. The other boys would be jealous of my sleuthing about. I was getting to have real action. Princess Reina would probably call me a hero. The thought made me smile.

We reached the house, and Ethan pushed himself into a crouch. Lansing and I stood but kept low. Ethan popped the hatch of the basement with no problem. There had been no lock. Beneath the opening was a layer of thick cobwebs lining the entrance, which we would have to move through in order to get into the basement. Something skittered below and made a squeaking sound. It was dark as night down there, impossible to see anything.

Ethan took point, pushing through the cobwebs to descend the steps. He accidentally kicked something metallic, which rolled across the basement floor until it clanged against the wall. All three of us froze. So much for not making noise. I drew my pistol, and I could see Lansing doing the same.

The floorboards *creaked* upstairs. It pained me to have to be silent, as I wanted to direct the others' attentions to it. My shoulders tensed, and I tightened my grip on my pistol. It was impossible to see anything down here.

A door opened above, not from the exterior where we'd come in, but from the direction we'd been slowly heading. All three of us trained pistols toward the door, but it didn't open all the way. Something dropped inside, bouncing off stairs. After three more bounces, it hit the floor. The door slammed shut, leaving us in darkness.

Whatever had been thrown in here made a hissing noise.

"Smoke bomb!" Ethan said. "Cover your faces and push forward.

He'll be expecting us to run out the way we came. We can use this to our advantage."

His plan sounded a little overly-aggressive, but he had more experience than me. The infantryman didn't protest.

I followed Ethan forward as quickly as I could. Smoke filled the room, and we rushed up the steps toward the main house. The old wood protested under my weight, flexing and groaning. It became harder to breathe. We'd have to get out soon.

Ethan hurried toward the door and jiggled on the handle. "It's sealed shut. We have to bust through."

"Shoot it," Lansing said. He coughed several times.

The smoke wasn't visible in the dark, but I definitely could smell it. My eyes watered, and I had to blink several times. I lifted the top of my tunic over my mouth and breathed through it.

Ethan fired several shots into the door. Something snapped, and he was able to push it open. "Come on," he said, charging into the house. Smoke flowed in his direction.

With the door open and light trickling in, I could finally see how immersed in smoke we were. A gray haze covered everything. Ethan rushed into the house and immediately ran for cover. There was no sign of the person who had thrown the smoke bomb. We were lucky he'd locked the door and decided to run.

Following Ethan, we crouched into what looked to be a kitchen area. Ethan knocked over a round table so it would shield us.

"You were right, he must have gone outside to try to pick us off when we exited the way we came," I said.

Ethan beamed with pride. "I thought that might be the case. Still no sign of any others. It might be us against the lone knight," Ethan said. "Okay, we'll check out the rest of the house and be ready for him once he comes back inside. Follow me."

Still maintaining our crouched positions, we spread out across the house. There wasn't much furniture in it. It was as barren as the exterior walls looked. Cobwebs lined the walls, old spills stained the floors. We moved to the room in the front of the house, where I recognized the boarded window with the sagging piece of wood, which allowed a view of trees in front of the house. The room was empty other than that. It had a stairwell leading to upstairs rooms, and the door leading out front, which was cracked open. Lou must have not shut it all the way when he went looking for us.

Even trying to be careful, the floorboards were so old and worn that they made noises with each step. I paused after a board creaked loudly underneath me. The others looked at me accusingly, but what could I have done to avoid it?

"Lou, that you?" a voice came from up the stairs.

Ethan motioned us to move the wall beside the stairwell so we would remain concealed. We tiptoed forward, trying not to make any further noise. There were other enemies here. That didn't bode well for us.

Footsteps came down the stairwell. "Lou?" the voice asked again.

I saw a large man through the railing. He hadn't looked in our direction yet, but we wouldn't remain hidden for long. Ethan apparently realized the same thing. He stood from his crouch and leveled his pistol at the man. *Click. Click. Click.*

No bullets flew from the gun, despite Ethan pulling on the trigger. The pistol chambers had been emptied. He must have unloaded too many shots into that door on our way out. I couldn't blame him. We'd needed to get out of there quickly.

"I need to reload," Ethan said quietly.

The gunshot noises alerted the large man on the stairs. He drew his own weapon and pointed it toward us.

We pressed our backs against the wall. He fired two bullets, which went into the floor. Lansing held his gun up above his head, firing blindly up above.

"Agh!" the man said. It must have hit him somewhere. Hard footsteps pounded down the stairway. When he rounded the corner, I could see the man was hopping on one foot. Blood seeped from his leg.

And now he stood exposed to us. Both Lansing and I fired at the attacker. Our bullets struck true, but he was still able to level his gun in our direction. He fired one last shot before he collapsed.

The bullet hit Lansing in the shoulder. Lansing crumpled to the floor in pain, his back against the wall.

"Oh no. Are you okay?" I asked, gingerly touching his good arm as he cradled his shoulder.

"I'll live. Hurts like none other." He clenched his teeth. "Stay on guard. There's a lot more fighting left to do. I'll keep."

I nodded.

Ethan had already made his way up the stairs. He had the rotary gun in his hands, ready for anyone else he might face. I followed him to the stairs, leaving Lansing alone.

When Ethan reached the top, some more scuffling came from upstairs. "Three rooms up here. Small bedrooms," Ethan said. "Cover me."

He trudged forward, long barrel pointed ahead of him. I hurried up the stairs so I could back him up. When I reached the landing, another man rushed out of the room to my right, tackling Ethan.

The big gun would be useless. The two men grappled. Ethan was slammed against the wall. I couldn't get a clear shot. Ethan struggled with the man, roughly equal in size, but older, and much dirtier looking. Who had Lou been consorting with? The man managed to punch Ethan in the face. His fist cracked on Ethan's cheekbone, jerking Ethan's head to the side. I winced.

Ethan didn't stagger and didn't pause to address his wound. He pushed the man against the opposite wall. The man's head snapped backward and crashed against the wood siding. He looked dazed. Seizing the moment, Ethan turned him in my direction, his attacker's body facing me. "Shoot!"

I blinked, not understanding he was speaking to me at first. Raising my pistol, I leveled it directly at them, but I hesitated. What if the bullet went through the man and hit Ethan? Or what if I missed?

"Do it now!" Ethan said. The man tried to move, clawing at Ethan's throat.

I fired.

The shot blasted directly into the man's back. He convulsed and fell in front of Ethan.

Ethan let out a deep breath, tapping the body with his toe to make sure the man was dead. "Good job. First lesson, when I tell you to do something, do it immediately. Don't delay."

Before I could respond, he turned to look into the three rooms up the stairs. He dismissed two of the rooms immediately. The third made his eyes go wide.

"What is it?" I asked.

Ethan turned back toward me. "Fearson. They got him." He didn't elaborate, but then again, he didn't need to. If his face was any indication, the scene inside the room wouldn't have been any prettier than the man sprawled out limply at the top of the stairs. I didn't need to see that. It pained my heart enough to think about Fearson being gone. Not that it would have been the first time I'd experienced such a death, but it also made me think of my parents, something I couldn't afford to do right now.

"It happens. Such is war," Ethan said, his tone softer than usual.

"Yeah. Let's take care of Lansing," I said.

I turned. Lou strode through the front door. Anger filled his eyes.

CHAPTER 16

I OPENED MY MOUTH TO WARN ETHAN, BUT BEFORE I DID, HE PUSHED ME down the stairs. I lost my balance. My pistol flew out of my hands. I rolled once on the steps, my body hitting the hard wood as I slid down the stairs. My jaw snapped shut, and I bit my lip in the process. Blood trickled into my mouth when my face hit the third step, salty and metallic. It wouldn't heal quickly.

I finally crashed against Lou's legs. He hadn't been expecting the maneuver and stumbled backward, tripping. He had twin pistols in his hands, but he dropped one of them during the collision. The other one shot into the ceiling. Wood splinters fell on top of my head. Looking back at Ethan, I saw bullet holes in the steps where I'd been standing. Ethan had saved me by giving me the push.

Ethan jumped the railing, landing beside Lansing. The infantryman offered Ethan a gun, but Ethan drew his sword instead. "Fight me like a knight, Lou!" he snarled at the turncoat. "Or do you remember how to, with your traitorous ways?"

Lou kicked my head like it was a ball, boot meeting my jaw and forcing me to the side. My body rolled over again, and I faced the ceiling this time. It spun above me, and bile rose in my throat. The knight stepped over me, drawing his sword. I wanted to help Ethan, but right now, I couldn't even stand up straight.

"Boy, I've watched your sword work. You're no match for me," Lou said.

Ethan laughed, almost maniacally. I'd never heard him like that before. His boots echoed on the creaky floor, edging toward me. The sound reverberated in my head, compounding the spinning and splitting my head. I tried to turn to see them, but my body wouldn't move.

Steel clashed against steel. And then again. Their steps and their sword work both moved at a furious pace.

"Ack!" Ethan yelped. Something crashed against the ground.

"Next time it's going to be right through your chest, boy," Lou said.

"I wanted you to knock that gun off me. It was slowing me down," Ethan quipped.

More sounds of swords reverberating against each other. What was Lansing doing?

I finally managed to turn onto my side. The spinning slowed, but I was still in a lot of pain. My head didn't feel right. From my new vantage, I could see the two men parrying each other's blows, both holding their grounds respectably. Lansing sat unmoving against the wall, a pool of blood formed under him. His eyes were closed, and his jaw open. He needed medical attention. Someone to stop the bleeding and get the bullet out of him. But I had no one to call for help. I could barely move, but I had to try.

Lou redoubled his attacks against Ethan. As the fight wore on, Lou's stamina proved to be a major factor. Ethan wasn't accustomed to prolonged sword fights as a knight of many years would be. Lou's strength began to overwhelm Ethan, who gave ground, step by step. Soon he was backed into a doorway, with very little room to maneuver.

The fight wouldn't last much longer. The momentum had swung, and Ethan had no way to recover. I had to do something before it was too late. Could I distract Lou somehow, at the very least?

I focused ahead of me, trying to keep the world steady and my nausea at bay. This was what Cid had spent all those hours training me for. I had the ability and the determination to get through this. I would prove myself worthy of being a knight.

Lou jabbed his sword toward Ethan, who swatted it with his own blade, pushing Lou's to the side. Every move Ethan made now was defense. Lou recovered his aim quickly and jabbed once more, the tip of his blade digging into Ethan's chest just above his breast.

It wasn't a fatal wound, but Ethan let out a guttural howl.

If I was going to help, I'd have to act quickly. I crawled across the floor toward the two of them. If Lou didn't take note of me, I could make it to the kitchen entryway and grab him by the foot. That would give Ethan the edge.

Those hopes were dashed as Lou apparently read my mind, or at least heard me coming. He swatted his sword behind him as if trying to warn me away before bringing it back to deliver another offensive assault. Ethan had sweat dripping down his face, and he was turning pale. Perhaps it was the wound, or perhaps he was growing wearier. Either way, I only had seconds left before Lou would finish him. I could sense it.

I scrambled toward them as best I could, my hands slapping on the floor, pain surging with every movement, though it didn't hurt any worse than my jaw, which had swollen shut since being kicked. It took almost all of my energy to push halfway through the room toward the two dueling men. I wasn't going to make it or affect the outcome of their battle.

Then, out the corner of my eye, I saw the rotary gun Ethan had dropped. It was nearly within reach. I shuffled on my belly to my left, scraping against the hard floor one last time. There was no time to think, Ethan was backing into the kitchen and would soon be pressed against the table we'd used as cover when we entered the house.

I pawed at the gun, pulling it closer to me. Hopefully there weren't any extra steps to work it beyond pulling the trigger. I hadn't seen anything different than a normal gun when Ethan fired it, but I didn't scrutinize his movements, either. The gun was heavy, and in my current condition, I struggled to maneuver it. I braced the butt of it on the floor and against my shoulder, pointing it through the doorway. Then I pulled the trigger.

The rotary gun whirred as its gears turned. I pointed it directly at Lou. But instead of firing, the gears *clacked* together. It didn't sound right. Metal came to a screeching halt within the automatic firing contraption. Smoke wafted from the aether reservoir. My finger was still depressing the trigger, but no bullets came out.

The gun was jammed.

Lou stabbed his sword toward Ethan, just missing to the side, but tearing his tunic. The ripping sound made Ethan's eyes go wide.

"Next one will be your insides," Lou taunted.

My head swam. I hurt so badly. But I couldn't just let Ethan die. If he died, I would, and Lansing would as well. Moreover, this traitor would be able to safely meet with his Wyranth associates. What would it mean for the kingdom?

I used the gun as a crutch, placing the back of it firmly on the ground, using it to lift myself to my feet. Everything spun in the room, but I kept my eyes focused ahead. I had to make a difference.

The two men parried blows twice more by the time I made it to my feet. It was a good thing I had the gun to hold me upright, or I would have never been able to stand. I spread my feet wide to try to keep my balance. Standing alone wouldn't do the trick. I needed to do more.

I clutched the rotary gun tightly. Lou was engaged, not focused on me. It was up to me if we were going to live.

Ethan backed into the wall. He was out of room. It was now or never.

I broke into a run—or at least as much as I could. It was more like stumbling forward, barely able to keep my balance. I dragged the gun with me, and brought it up like a club.

Lou turned, hearing the movement behind him, but there was little he could do. I brought the gun down hard, whacking him in the shoulder. It made a *crack* sound when it hit bone.

Lou turned pale from the pain, dropping his sword. I'd connected very well.

Ethan didn't waste a moment, and by the time Lou turned back, he'd rammed his sword directly through Lou's belly. The tip protruded out his back.

I couldn't keep my balance any longer, and I crashed hard to the floor. My jaw hit the wood planks, causing me to lose my vision for a moment. When my sight returned, Lou had dropped to his knees in front of me, clutching at his stomach.

Ethan pulled his sword out of Lou, the blade covered in red.

The pain from falling to the floor hit me harder than anything so far. I reeled, but my jaw was puffing up so badly I couldn't open my mouth to scream.

Lou collapsed to the floor, a pool of blood forming around him. Ethan stepped over him, heading toward me. He sheathed his sword. Though his tunic was cut to shreds, and he bled from the one wound near his chest, the cuts didn't seem to bother him. "Your face is all puffed up like a fish!" Ethan laughed heartily. "But at least you got to use the rotary gun, right? Now you won't have to give me those jealous stares anymore."

I didn't find it terribly funny. Nor did I feel like I'd really been able to use the gun. Next time, I vowed I would in earnest. But we had more pressing matters to attend to. "Lansing...stop...bleeding..." I managed to slur.

Ethan looked to Lansing and frowned, his jovial attitude disappearing. "I'm on it," he said, moving over to the infantryman. He crouched and tore some fabric from Lansing's tunic, tying it into a knot to try to stop the bleeding. "I can't get the bullet out now. We'll have to find a doctor in Loveridge."

It sounded like a good idea, but my head throbbed. My focus all but evaporated. The blows to my skull were too much. My eyes closed, and I lost consciousness.

EPILOGUE

IN THE AFTERMATH OF OUR BATTLE AGAINST LOU AND HIS HENCHMEN, Ethan rushed to Loveridge, where he was able to find a doctor. They rode back in a carriage. When they arrived, they tended to Sergeant Lansing before reviving me with smelling salts. The doctor brought ice for my jaw and told me to relax for a couple of days before taking on any strenuous activity. I was getting sick of that routine from doctors. So many days out of commission.

We waited in Loveridge while we healed for four more days. Once Lansing and I could walk around again, we buried Fearson and our fallen enemies with the assistance of the locals. We'd sent a courier to deliver Cid the news that we had completed our mission and needed some time to heal. Once we were ready to leave ourselves, Ethan conscripted a civilian carriage cab from the town so we wouldn't have to walk back to Rislandia City. "It'll be at the expense of the knights," he said, almost too happily.

The ride was relaxing, as much as the road was bumpy. Minor complaints aside, I was happy not to be on my feet after days of traveling and running. I could finally speak again, which made things a little easier, though I found I was too weary to have much conversation.

We arrived after a full day's ride, after stopping to retrieve our belongings from our camp. I found I actually missed my dormitory bed, as much as I never would have thought it. Sleeping away from Tristan's snoring was almost too quiet.

A knight greeted us in the courtyard, and Ethan explained what happened. The knight gave the driver his fare, and we walked back toward the spire. We agreed to rest for the evening, after the day of travel, and give Cid a report in the morning. I bid Ethan and Lansing a good night and moved toward the apprentice dormitory.

I still walked slowly, though I tried to hide any of my pain so I wouldn't limp in front of the others. They would give me enough grief over the mission as it was. In a strange, fortuitous moment, a large shadow eclipsed the sun. I stopped to look up, hearing an unmistakable *whirring* noise. An airship glided overhead, the glass portholes in its wooden hull glistening when it passed. *The Liliana.* Our kingdom's only flying machine.

Zair-bear must have been returning from a mission, just as I was. Part of me wanted to go see her, to see how she was doing. Really, I just wanted to talk to her. But it was strange now. It'd only been a couple of months, but I found myself at a loss as to what I would say. Our worlds had become so different. My life was as an apprentice to the Crystal Spire now. She had her own problems, and didn't need to hear mine. I couldn't imagine she'd be as understanding as Princess Reina, but then, I didn't think the princess would be either. Whatever happened, when I saw Zair-bear again, it would be far too complicated.

I sighed to myself.

The night breeze picked up with that thought, making me shiver. It made me feel alone. It was probably just because I was tired. A good night's sleep, and I'd be in better shape.

I returned to my dormitory and fell asleep almost instantly. I was awakened early by other boys shaking me. All three of my bunkmates were at my bed.

"What was the mission like? Still got time for any of us lowly apprentices?" asked Albert, a redheaded boy who had the bunk across from me.

"Let him wake up," Tristan said.

I stretched, and sat up in my bed. It didn't feel like I'd had a good night's sleep at all. I could have used several more hours, but the other boys wouldn't let me be. I told them my story as we dressed for the day and went to breakfast.

"You swung a gun like a club," Tristan said, sounding unimpressed.

"More than you got to do after the competition," Albert said.

Did he just defend me from Tristan's jealousy? Maybe things would start to get better around here after all.

"I need to go get my porridge," I said, jutting a thumb toward the food counter.

"Come sit with us after," Albert said. "I want to hear more."

After breakfast, my routine returned to normal with classes and training from the master knights. I probably could have taken the day off, but I wanted to be occupied and among others. Isolating myself didn't seem to be a good idea after my prior evening's thoughts.

The whole day passed without Cid's summons. It was another two days before he found me and brought me to his office. Ethan was there, and he recounted the story on my behalf, talking up my abilities far more than I thought I deserved credit for.

"He probably saved mine and Sergeant Lansing's life," Ethan said.

Cid's forehead wrinkled as he considered. "A good report. James, you're going to go places in the knights. I can see this already. And speaking of which, I have another mission for the both of you. Zaira von Monocle has convinced the king to send an expedition over to the Zicree continent."

"All the way over the Golgmarsh Ocean?" I asked.

Cid nodded. "It's likely to be dangerous, and the king asked for knights to assist with the mission. I need all of our master knights out on patrol, but with how you handled the Lou situation, I believe you'll both be more than capable. Ethan can mentor you during the journey to the other continent, and I believe you already work well with the *Liliana's* crew?"

My lips crept upward into a beaming smile. To be on an airship again! Even if it would be awkward with Zair-bear, which I wasn't sure it would be, I couldn't wait for the prospect. And I liked working with Ethan. This would be the best of all worlds for me. Finally, things were looking up in my life as an apprentice knight.

"You bet!"

<<<<>>>>

PART II
GUARD TRAINING

RISLANDIAN TIMELINE NOTES

The events in this story take place during The Fight For Rislandia, *beginning after Chapter Nine.*

CHAPTER 1

THE *LILIANA* TOOK OFF FROM THE GRASSY AREA WHERE THE ENORMOUS airship had landed earlier. A large shadow fell over me and close to a dozen others standing nearby, wind picking up as the giant propellers turned at incredible speeds. Princess Reina's hair flew in her face, and she quickly brushed it away.

King Malaky motioned for everyone to follow him. Quiet tension created an uneasiness between everyone. The unspoken question hung in the air—would the Kingdom of Rislandia still exist in the coming days?

I couldn't be sure. It boggled my mind that the Grand Rislandian Army would evacuate King Malaky and his entourage from Rislandia City. The Wyranth army had been making substantive advances in the last few days, coming in numbers I could hardly fathom, but it felt like we'd given up.

As the group walked toward the sprawling estate to the east, I snuck a glance at Princess Reina, King Malaky's daughter and sole heir to the throne. She may have requested me as a bodyguard, but the real reason she wanted me there was because she enjoyed sneaking kisses with me in the moonlight. She hadn't stated it, of course, but Ma didn't raise James Gentry to be a fool.

I may not have had the best track record with women so far, but she *liked* me. At least, she liked kissing me. Either way, I'd take it.

We came to the main gates of the residence, a structure similar to the main palace in Rislandia City, made from massive stone bricks. Two towers adorned the front before a pair of gates that led inside. Long walls stretched left and right.

The gates opened, revealing a courtyard inside with two square patches of flowers and a walkway down the middle to a rear structure. The back structure's walls were made of glass both on this side and on the other, providing a view of both the room inside and a deck that hung over the cliff, where the palace was built, to Lake Avily beyond. A fire lit the interior room where servants scrambled for last-minute cleaning.

Servants opened the big glass doors as King Malaky stomped toward them. The king's mood trickled to everyone around me— Princes Reina, Mr. du Gearsmith, a couple of attendants, and more guards. I recognized the guards as my fellow knights. Reggie, an apprentice like me, and one who didn't like me very much, Tanner, a journeyman with a little tuft of hair under his bottom lip, and Handley, a stockier journeyman knight with dark hair.

We entered the large, open room. King Malaky immediately moved to a place where he could look out over the lake. He clasped his hands behind his back. The others stayed behind him, giving the king his space to brood. What could we do? How could we begin to console him?

King Malaky turned to his servants. "Make sure everyone is set up in quarters. We may be here for a while. When is the Atreblan ambassador set to arrive?"

"Tomorrow, your Majesty," Mr. du Gearsmith said.

King Malaky nodded. "I hope tomorrow's not too late."

"The von Monocles will defend the city," Mr. du Gearsmith replied.

"I wish I had your faith. Theo and Zaira have done so much for us, but I don't see a way we can come out victorious this time. We've allowed this threat to go on for so long." King Malaky clenched his fist. "I should have been stronger when they killed my father. I should have pressed the fight then."

"All you can affect is the future, your Majesty," Mr. du Gearsmith said. "You are a man of peace. You didn't want war, and you offered a good solution that was appropriate at the time. They betrayed *you*." His voice was firm, with clear emotional support for the king.

King Malaky frowned and nodded. "Yes, perhaps you're right."

Mr. du Gearsmith clapped his hands. "You heard the king. Let's get our faithful knights and guests their quarters. There's a lot of work to do yet."

The servants turned and made their way toward the west wing of the estate, passing a door by the fire. Reggie, Tanner, and Handley followed. Reina started to move as well, but King Malaky held a hand up. "Reina, stay with me."

I inclined my head, not sure what I should do, since I was supposed to guard the princess. Should I be following the other knights?

"You're dismissed, Mr. Gentry," King Malaky said, answering my unspoken question.

I nodded and jogged to catch up with the others.

"Reina, I wanted to talk to you about the position you put me in on the *Liliana*," King Malaky said.

"Hmm?" Reina asked, sounding as innocent as ever.

I didn't mean to eavesdrop, but the sound echoed in the open room with stone floor. What could I do?

"Bringing the boy, Gentry, here. I choose our guard retinue. It was a foolish thing to do and unbecoming of a princess."

"James has been nothing but helpful to the kingdom."

"Reina, I've seen you close to him. You're fraternizing with that boy. He's a commoner. If we weren't in the middle of a crisis, whispers of scandal would be reaching the entire kingdom."

"I don't care. He's nice, and I like him."

"I want you to stay away from him."

I dragged my feet those last few steps. I wanted to hear more. He was talking about me. Worse, he spoke about me with *her!* When I was with Reina, I didn't think of anything except for the way her beautiful blonde hair fell over her shoulders, or the way her blue eyes twinkled when they looked at me. This talk about propriety and commoners... it wasn't my world. I bit my lip as I followed the others through the hallway. Should I not be spending time with Princess Reina? Was it a foolish endeavor?

This was all so confusing. I'd finally worked out all my feelings with Zaira, realized we were just friends, and part of it had been because I liked Reina so much. But there was a lot more to consider. She had responsibilities as heir to the throne of Rislandia. I was just a nobody from Plainsroad Village. Of course the king didn't want me around her. He probably needed her to marry some dignitary or another from a foreign government to secure relations. That's how it worked with these noble types, right?

Truthfully, I had no idea how it worked. All I knew was that my chest stung when faced with the prospect of losing Reina. I'd barely had any time to get to know her! It didn't help that we spent most of our time kissing when we should have been talking. But I liked kissing. She liked kissing. What was the problem?

"James!" Reggie snapped his fingers in front of my face to pull me from my thoughts.

I lingered in the hallway, with two servants who were trying to usher us into a room with two small bunks. "Yeah?" I asked.

"This is where we're staying. Set your stuff down."

I dropped my pack and sat on the bed. It was a little too mushy of a mattress for my liking. Our beds back at the Crystal Spire had a wonderful firmness to them.

"Your turn for the washroom will be in an hour, after the journeymen have had their chance," said one of the servants.

I nodded. They departed.

"What are you daydreaming about, Gentry?" Reggie asked. "You'd better shape up if you're going to be the princess's guard. She's a prime target for assassination just like King Malaky. I bet you anything the Wyranth will try to send someone here."

Assassination? Of course. That was why they had knights to guard the royal family in the first place. I felt like I'd reneged in my duties for worrying about how I was going to sneak more kisses with the princes when I should have been focused on keeping her safe. The more I thought about it, the more King Malaky had a point in saying it was a terrible idea to have me guarding her. But he didn't know the half of it. I didn't know if I could focus around her, other than focusing on the delightful way her hips curved. I could stare at her all day long, but I needed to be aware of what went on around her. "You're right," I said under my breath.

"I am?" Reggie blinked as if he'd just seen a ghost. "Now I know something's wrong. You've never thought I was right since you started with the knights." He unpacked his items in his bag and placed them in a drawer. "Well, hopefully you'll get back to normal if anything bad happens here. I don't like you, Gentry, but we need you if we're gonna survive this."

It seemed like it'd been so long since the days I'd first become an apprentice. Reggie had been foolish, hurting other kids in tournaments to get ahead. I didn't like that, but we'd spent so much time apart since then, with my traveling to the Zenwey continent and getting stuck there for months. He'd been fighting on the front lines against the Wyranth invasion. We weren't kids anymore. Everything changed so fast I hardly could keep up.

CHAPTER 2

I COULDN'T SLEEP VERY WELL IN THE BUNK. REGGIE SNORED, BUT MY restless night was due to more than my roommate's sleeping noises. All I could think about was how I didn't belong here, how I *couldn't* belong here. I didn't get recruited to the knights to be a palace guard, or Princess Reina's personal guard. I should have been out in the action, defending Rislandia.

The king didn't want me here. He viewed me as a peasant boy who distracted his daughter from the important things. Worse, he was right.

I tossed and turned all night between those roaring snores. When I woke in the morning, my eyes were bloodshot. I could hardly be called alert enough to be a guard.

Tanner caught sight of me in the morning, and he handed me a cup of a steaming liquid.

"What's this?" I asked.

"Coffee. It'll pick you up," he said.

I'd heard of coffee, but I'd never seen it before. Out on the farm in Plainsroad Village, we didn't have access to a lot of luxuries, and when we traveled on the airship, the crew only drank tea and beer. Coffee beans were grown out in Perryton, and while they weren't a rarity, they were an expensive import.

I took the cup in my hands. It was warm, almost too hot with the liquid steaming into my face. Not wanting to be rude, I took a sip.

It was the most bitter, awful thing I'd ever tasted. I made a disgusted face.

Tanner laughed. "C'mon, it's much easier to swallow than spirits."

I opened my mouth to tell him I'd never drunk alcohol, but Tanner had already turned to leave the kitchen area. The brown liquid swished in the cup, daring me to drink more. I wrinkled my nose and slurped. It wasn't as bad on the second sip.

"James, we're going to need you," I heard Reina call from down the hallway.

Time to work. The coffee was too hot just to guzzle quickly, but I did my best to finish as much as I could with careful sips. I had to find somewhere to put it down, so I stashed it on one of the countertops. Hopefully, the servants wouldn't be too annoyed. I straightened my tunic and rushed toward the main greeting room.

King Malaky was there, along with Mr. du Gearsmith. The two men conversed in low tones, solemn expressions on their faces. Reina stood by the fire, turning to me and beaming when she saw me. She wore a long dress, a dark green that made her skin appear all the more pale against it. The tips of her hair fell over her chest perfectly, as if they were part of the emerald necklace she wore.

It took everything in me not to drop my jaw and gawk at her. But I had to remain stoic. I kept my lips clamped shut, as a guard should.

"Hello, James," Reina said as I entered. The two men behind her raised their heads. King Malaky furrowed his brow disapprovingly.

What had I walked into?

"I don't expect there will be any security issues with the Atreblan Ambassador," King Malaky said, "but we'll have an honor guard all the same. James, you'll stand in the corner of the room with the others." He pointed across from Reina, about as far as one could get. Was he giving me a hint beyond mere orders? I'd heard the political types often made subtle gestures to try to get their points across.

It might have been paranoia. "Yes, your Majesty," I said and made my way across the room.

I took my position by Reggie, Tanner, and Handley, who was the last to arrive. We stood in a row, erect at attention, eyes scanning but ever looking ahead.

King Malaky and Mr. du Gearsmith resumed their conversation, leaving the guards with little to do for a good amount of time. I couldn't get a glimpse of the small clock on the fireplace mantle. The hands looked fuzzy, and it wasn't a big clock. Or so I told myself.

Ethan von Lantern, a journeyman who'd played a big role in my training, had once told me I might need spectacles. I hoped not. Glasses would be so cumbersome, and a knight would look ridiculous wearing them.

Minutes passed. We stood still and at attention. Guard duty was the worst. I liked to be out adventuring. The other apprentices tended to get jealous over how much I was able to skip the regular schooling and gallivant on an airship. I wondered if I'd ever be able to do so again. Not that it was terrible being around Reina, but I preferred *doing* things.

I found myself getting restless. I wanted to tap my feet, scratch an itch under my right eye, go run down by the lake—anything! No one had arrived. Even though I'd had breakfast, my stomach rumbled. I just wanted to move.

It was the coffee. Tanner had told me it would pick me up. It put my mind through loops. I couldn't remember having so much energy, and even though standing there was boring, it couldn't account for how much of a need I had to jump up in the air and do cartwheels.

I started to sing to myself in my head. I wouldn't make a noise and distract the king. My mother used to hum a tune as she peeled carrots back home. I still remembered the words.

O'er in the Dragonmist Isles,
the dragons they did ride.
Up and down the coastal shores,
until they up 'n died.

It was a morbid song, now that I thought about it. Yet it had such a happy tune. Why did parents sing things like that to their kids? I could never understand adults.

The front door swung open.

All of the guards held perfectly still. We had to appear more polished than ever. One of the servants cleared his throat. "Announcing Ambassador Sheila McRose of Atrebla and her retinue."

Several men in suits removed their top hats and entered. They positioned themselves to stand beside us. They didn't look like us as guards in our leathery knight garb. Their formal wear didn't appear the best for fighting, but I could tell they carried pistols under their coats by the way they bulged to the sides of their clothing. These were the ambassador's guards as much as we were King Malaky's.

The woman who followed them had a long, flowing dress, which she held up as she walked. It was the same color green as Princess Reina's, which the woman appeared to notice, stopping before the princess with an awkward stare. While she was an elegant woman with a round face, I much preferred Princess Reina's figure in her dress.

"Well, it seems green's the fashion," Ambassador McRose said coolly.

"Indeed," Reina said, taking a more formal tone to her voice than I was used to hearing. She lifted her chin proudly.

I could never understand women. Why they acted like two barn cats ready to brawl over a dress color was beyond me. I kept my face expressionless all the same. I didn't want to draw attention to myself.

King Malaky cleared his throat. "Ambassador, it's good to see you."

McRose curtsied before the king. "King Malaky, a pleasure. It's been a long time."

"Sadly, the state of affairs in Rislandia this last year has had me preoccupied. I am sad I missed our annual gathering in Edmon."

"I, as well. Rislandia brings the life of the party. I hear Theo von Monocle's returned?" She cocked an eyebrow up higher on her forehead than I would have thought possible on the woman.

"Yes," King Malaky said. "Though he's currently on a mission."

"As always. His exploits are known far and wide. The greatest adventurer who ever lived, or the wiliest devil, depending on who you speak with."

"Perhaps a little of both," King Malaky said. His eyes twinkled very similarly to the way Reina's often did. The look startled me. "Please, would you have a seat?" King Malaky motioned to one of the leather chairs before the fire.

McRose nodded, lifted her skirts again so she could smooth them as she took the chair. "I do love my visits to Lake Avily. It's so elegant here."

"It's one of my favorite places to rest and deliberate on important matters. Would you care for a glass of wine?"

"Please. The journey's long, and Atrebla doesn't have the air travel available to us that's at your disposal," she said.

King Malaky took a seat in the chair next to her, while Princess Reina sat beside him, hands folded in her lap, listening, smiling, and laughing where appropriate through the idle conversation. I'd never get used to the stuffy formalities of royal society.

Servants had wine glasses at the ready within moments, as well as a platter with cheeses and cured meats for the ambassador. They made my stomach grumble all the more. Some of the cheeses were so pungent, I could smell them from across the room.

In some ways, Reina had the same job I did—to sit still and be observant. While my face was flat, hers was cheerful, but otherwise, she was very much a background prop in the play King Malaky was presenting to the ambassador. It amazed me how much they talked about nothing significant. Weather. The lake. Modern art styles and horseless carriages. I was ready to fall asleep by the time they came down to serious business.

"I asked you here to speak about the war," King Malaky said.

McRose brought her wine glass to her lips, the red liquid nearly empty after her long sip. "I assumed so. Our informers have brought back reports that show it's going... How do I put this delicately...?"

"There's no need," King Malaky said, his forehead wrinkling. He looked so tired, so old. It broke my heart to see him like this. "It's been disastrous. We're on the verge of losing Rislandia City."

McRose had been reaching for another slice of cheese, but she stopped herself. "Oh, my. I'm sorry. I hadn't realized it was *that* bad."

"No need for apologies. But we are in a desperate situation, and we need your help. If Atrebla could provide food, supplies, and I'd ask for troops, but..." King Malaky shook his head.

"I can tell you right now King Eakin won't send an armed force. We already have enough trouble with the goblins along our northern countryside by Zarma."

"They've returned? I thought Theo—"

"That was more than a decade ago."

King Malaky frowned. "Time's gone so quickly. And I'm afraid if matters go as they are now, we'll have very little of it left for Rislandia. Surely King Eakin doesn't wish to have the Iron Emperor's fist at his southern border? He knows the Wyranth are far more dangerous than goblins can ever be."

McRose grimaced. "Spoken like someone who's never come into contact with one of the foul beasts. But I'll forgive the unintended slight. Yes, we are aware of how dangerous the Wyranth have become. We're also aware of the soldier serum that's made their men so aggressive."

"We're developing ways to counteract that. And we'll need time. It's for everyone on the Areth continent's benefit that we succeed," King Malaky said. His voice was coaxing, soothing. It made me want to do everything I could to help him. But, I would've anyway. Why wouldn't McRose offer help?

She pursed her lips and looked to Princess Reina. "You've flourished quite a bit in recent years, Reina. I believe King Eakin has a son about your age."

Reina stiffened, eyes darting to her father.

"I... Such matters would be up to Princess Reina," King Malaky said. I'd never seen him look so uncomfortable.

I'd never been so uncomfortable either. It took everything in me not to shout at the ambassador and let her know Reina was mine. It was a foolish emotion, though. Sure, we'd shared a few kisses, but I couldn't claim ownership over Reina, could I?

My heart nearly pounded out of my chest as I thought about it. I didn't want to lose her because of a negotiation. Why did everything have to fall apart so quickly?

McRose laughed. "It's always surprised me how you allowed your subjects so much of their own will. Granting your nobles their airships, for example? Absurd. They should be the kingdom's property."

"Reina isn't my subject," King Malaky said firmly.

"Father..." Reina whispered.

"It's true. I am teaching you all I know. You're my daughter. I love you. The kingdom will be yours one day, and I value you as an equal."

McRose smiled. "A noble sentiment, to be certain. But I was getting to another point. While it would be nice to match King Eakin's son with such a delightful young girl, the airships are what I'm here to speak with you about. Atrebla is more than twice the size of Rislandia, and travel can take a long time." It's a lot for a king as old as Eakin." She swirled her wine in her glass and took the last sip. "If there were a way for him to fly across the country in mere hours, it would ease his burdens considerably."

"We can offer transport, within reason, once this war is over," King Malaky said.

"While a generous offer, we need more control over the king's schedule. You understand." McRose set her glass down and met King Malaky's eyes with hers.

King Malaky frowned. "You're asking a lot of us."

"These are trying times." McRose shrugged.

I didn't like her. I wanted to wring her neck. How dare she talk to the king like that? We needed supplies. Our troops might run out of food if we weren't careful, and she wanted to play games with airships?

King Malaky didn't betray any anger if he felt the same way as I did. Instead, he stood. "Such a large request, it'll have to be something we discuss more than just this meeting. I have to deliberate and speak to my advisors."

"Of course," McRose said, standing.

"Shall we break and take a stroll around the lake?" King Malaky asked.

"I would very much enjoy that," McRose said.

Mr. du Gearsmith, who had been over by us, motioned to us to move. The other guards turned and headed out the back door of the cabin. I followed. The Atreblan ambassador's party joined us. Even though King Malaky did his best to keep the outing light, the heavy mood weighed on all of us.

Storm clouds formed above the mountains in the north.

CHAPTER 3

AFTER A PLEASANT STROLL ALONG THE LAKE, WITH REINA SNEAKING FAR too many glances at me in front of her father to be comfortable for me, we returned to the king's retreat. The fire made the main room nice and warm, in contrast to the crisp autumn air outside. Mr. du Gearsmith offered to take the ambassador to her quarters and to play a game with her so they could catch up on personal matters. By the way McRose's eyes shimmered back at him, I suspected there had been more between them than a simple acquaintance.

They departed to the east guest wing with her guards, leaving the Rislandians together. Everyone waited in silence as the footsteps of the Atreblans pattered down the hall and disappeared behind a closing door.

King Malaky let out what looked like was a breath he'd been holding a while and paced to the fire. "I don't see how we can possibly give them airship technology. We've kept it a closely guarded secret for all of these years. Rislandia is the only kingdom to be able to fly around the world, and I think it's best to keep it that way," he said.

"I'm inclined to agree," Reina said, watching her father. "But what else can we do?"

King Malaky turned to her. "Sheila implied the potential of

marriage to the Atreblan Prince Gregor. I know you aren't fond of the idea, but we should be considering it. Such an arrangement could take the burden off the country for the airship technology."

Reina's eyes darted toward me. I tried my best not to react, but my stomach tensed into knots.

"No, I can't do that, Father. You know I won't. I want to stay in Rislandia. Besides, I'm your only heir. What would happen if I was whisked away to Atrebla?" Reina said.

I found I had been holding my breath similarly to the way King Malaky had been moments prior. I didn't sigh in relief because it would have been noticed, but I let the breath out slowly. Why was I so nervous about this? I hadn't even thought of the arguments Reina had against the marriage. I'd thought King Malaky respecting her decisions would have been enough. But those were good points.

"Mmm," King Malaky said, turning back to the fire. "I'm not sure what to do. I wish we had more time."

The main door opened. A short man with black hair entered. He wore one of the most finely-tailored suits I'd ever seen. It fell about perfectly on him. A gold chain dangled from his breast pocket, which I assumed carried a pocket watch inside. He held a handle, by which he dragged luggage on two wheels behind him.

"Your Majesty," the man said as servants came to help him with his luggage—which appeared very heavy by the way one struggled lifting it over the threshold—and to close the door behind him. "I apologize for not being in the proper attire."

King Malaky strode over to the man, all smiles. "Propriety flew out the window when this war heated up." He shook the man's hand, and then turned to us. "Everyone, I'd like to introduce you to Dr. Philip von Breech. He's one of the kingdom's expert scientists and is responsible for many of the inventions the knights have used in recent missions. Philip, meet knights James Gentry, Reginald Walther, David Tanner, and Joshua Handley," he said, motioning to us. "Of course, you know my daughter."

"How do you do?" said Dr. von Breech. "Good to see you again, Princess."

"And you," Reina said.

"I was on my way to Rislandia City from my lab in Brighton when a soldier in a horseless carriage stopped me. He said the Wyranth were at the city gates, and he was stationed to turn anyone back who might be heading southwest. The Wyranth are this far into the country?"

"I'm afraid so," King Malaky said.

"Terrible." Dr. von Breech shook his head. "I should have packed more from my estate, then. I can't have them raiding my lab if they make it further." He bit his lip. "There will be time for that later, I suppose. I wanted to speak with you directly, see if you required any assistance."

"Not unless you can create four more airships as we had in the past, and do so instantaneously," King Malaky said.

"Alas, I'm afraid not. But I do have some items you might find useful." He leaned over his luggage and opened up the case.

I was hoping for another automatic gun like the one Ethan and I had on our last outing as knights, but he produced something that looked to be some sort of lantern with a crank, and a strange leather piece, which looked like an arm-guard, but with all kinds of electronic devices on it. Switches, gears, a small exhaust.

"What have we here?" King Malaky asked.

"First." Dr. von Breech held up the lantern. He rapidly turned the crank, and the lantern shone brightly. He kept it going for a few seconds, but then let it turn off. "It's called a flashlight. It should prove useful in the dark. Saves the trouble of making a fire, and it can be used repeatedly without fuel due to the electricity generated in the crank."

"Impressive," King Malaky said.

"This," Dr. von Breech said, holding up the arm-guard, "is an aether-fueled auto-electrocuter."

That sounded dangerous. I wanted to try it. I fought back the urge to blurt out the question and ask. Cid and the other knights got annoyed enough when I spoke up and asked to use their devices back at the Crystal Spire. It probably wouldn't be a good idea to interrupt the king when he spoke with his scientist.

"I won't pretend to know what that means," King Malaky said with a chuckle.

"It's a weapon."

"Ah," King Malaky said. "Well, I'm sure one of our four knights here would love to assist in a demonstration."

Pick me. Pick me. Pick me.

King Malaky turned to us.

Dr. von Breech glanced between us along with the king. "It's best to be tried outdoors," he said.

"Let's head outside, then. James, why don't you try it out?"

Yes! I tried my hardest to look professional and not smile. "I'd be happy to, your Majesty."

We all went outside and stood in front of a pile of cut wood.

"Is this wood important, Your Majesty?" Dr. von Breech asked.

"It will serve for the demonstration," King Malaky said.

Dr. von Breech held the auto-electrocuter under his arm and pulled it out, loosening the straps so he could place it over my arm. "Hold your arm out," he said. I did as he said, and he secured it so tightly on me I could feel it cutting off my circulation.

"I think it's too tight," I said.

"You won't want to risk it being loose," he said.

I nodded.

"Do you feel the lever under your index and middle fingers?" he asked.

"Yes," I said.

"Great. It'll take the strength of both of your fingers to activate it. Point at your target."

I held my arm toward the wood pile. "Like this?"

"Step a little closer. It's only got a range of about four feet. Everyone else, give him a wide berth. We don't want to risk any injury from recoil or any problems with the auto-electrocuter." Dr. von Breech backpedaled toward the others.

I shuffled closer to the wood.

"Go ahead," Dr. Von Breech said.

I depressed the lever onto my palm. The brass lever was cold to the touch, but my arm heated up as the device shook, its gears activating. Exhaust *whooshed* from the back of it, warm steam on my shoulder. Then it fired.

A jolt of electricity blasted from atop my hand. It hit the woodpile, blasting it to splinters. The resulting force made me jerk my arm back.

"Don't keep holding the lever down or you might hit us!"

I released the lever, and the lightning stopped. My heart raced through the whole demonstration. So much power coming from my arm, such destruction. My eyes went wide. "This is crazy," I said.

"Maybe so, but it can be a powerful tool."

King Malaky nodded. "Your inventions are wondrous as always, Dr. von Breech. It makes me think…we might have something to offer the Atreblans after all."

"Are you sure?" Princess Reina asked.

"I'm not sure, but I'm sure we need their help if Rislandia's going to survive."

CHAPTER 4

"I want to go for a walk," Reina announced after dinner. All of us were gathered in the dining room. Between the guards and King Malaky's guests, it made for quite a sizable banquet table. We'd had a good meal of baked chicken.

"We've already gone around the lake today, Reina," King Malaky said from the head of the table, setting down his utensils. "I'd prefer to turn in early."

"Me as well," McRose said, dabbing a napkin on her lips.

King Malaky nodded as if that settled it.

Reina's eyes lit up in defiance. "It's fine. We'll use Dr. von Breech's flashlight. Won't we, James?"

I blinked at being put on the spot in front of everyone. "I…uh…"

"Reina," King Malaky warned.

"Let's go," Reina said to me without hesitation. She stood from the table, brandishing a warm—but fake—smile. "Dinner was lovely. My compliments." She curtsied in her dress and swept from the room.

"You'd better follow her," Tanner whispered to me.

I wiped my fingers on the napkin and stood. "Uh, yes. Dinner was very nice. Thank you." I bowed to the king and took off after Reina.

By the time I reached the main room, Reina had her coat on and stood at the back glass door. She held out a jacket to me in outstretched arms. I took the coat from her and shuffled into it. Then I grabbed my sword and holstered it at my belt. She opened the door, and we stepped outside into the evening breeze. My eyes watered from the cold, dry air. I hadn't expected it to be so brisk. I clutched my coat a little more tightly around me.

Reina didn't seem to mind the cold. She strolled at a casual pace until sure we were out of earshot from the house. "It's been so miserable as of late."

"I know," I said, keeping pace at her side.

"I'm sorry my father is so stuffy. As much as he's a kind king, he still holds prejudices about commoners. It can't be helped. It doesn't influence me at all, so you know."

"I know. It's okay. I'm just here to keep you safe."

Reina laughed and patted my arm. "I like how innocent you are."

"Thanks?" I said, half-smiling at her.

We traveled the dirt path along the shore of the lake. Clouds blotted out the sky completely, revealing no stars, no moon. Everything was lifeless. I shivered.

"I know we're in the worst of times, but I want to have a life, too," Reina said. "There's no one to talk to here, none of my friends. Except you. I wanted you along so I could talk."

I figured it would be best to let her do just that. My Da always told me it was better to listen to women when they wanted to talk. Seemed like a good idea when I didn't know what to say.

"And I don't know what to do with ambassadors or politics or a war." Reina motioned toward the southwest. "I know he's training me to lead Rislandia by having me along, but what am I supposed to do?"

The words hung in the air. I bit my lip before replying timidly, "Pay attention?"

Reina slapped me on the arm.

"Hey!" I said, recoiling and acting like the slap injured me far more than it did.

Her eyes went wide. "I didn't mean to hit you that hard. But that was an idiotic comment, James Gentry."

"You asked," I said, shrugging.

She rubbed my arm for me. Even through the thick jacket, I enjoyed her touch. We both stopped walking and faced each other. I wasn't sure what to do. Should I put my hands on her waist? Would that be too forward of me? We'd kissed before, but I still wasn't exactly sure where I stood with her. Did kissing her mean I had permission to kiss her again? She confused me so much.

Reina's head turned to the side, stopping any thoughts I might have had of making a move. "I just wanted to have fun. I don't know why my father has to butt his head into everything and make it complicated."

"At least you have a father."

I didn't mean to say that. I wished I'd said anything but. The words came out sounding so bitter, and it made my chest feel like it contracted in on itself. I found I could barely breathe in the cold air. What was wrong with me?

Reina frowned, backing away from me. "James, I'm sorry, I didn't mean..."

"I know," I said, my lip quivering. By Malaky, I couldn't fall apart here. Not in front of her. Not like this. I'd managed to ignore my parents' death for almost a year. Now I couldn't think of anything else.

Sounds in the distance only made matters worse. The Wyranth war contraptions *clacked* much like the sound of breaking twigs in the forest. An animal must have stepped on one. It echoed. A bird who hadn't migrated for the coming winter took off into the sky. It flew, just like I'd fled that evening.

I clutched my chest. The pain was too much. My eyes started to water.

"James, are you okay?" Reina asked.

"No..." I managed to blurt out.

My parents were gone. My best friend, the girl I'd always thought I'd end up with until I met Reina, was off on another mission on her airship, with an attachment of her own, no less.

I was all alone. If I lost Reina because I couldn't keep my emotions in check, I'd never be able to live with myself. Why now? Tears streaked down my eyes.

"You never had time to grieve," Reina said, speaking almost as much to herself as she did to me. "It's just been one crisis to the next. Poor James," she said, returning closer me to give me an embrace.

"No." I gave her a light push to her arm. "I don't want you to feel bad for me. I want you to like me because I'm worthy."

Reina's countenance became one of extreme confusion and sadness. Her eyes seemed to droop in a way I'd never seen them do before. I hated seeing her like that. I wanted her to be happy. "Worthy? I like you because you're you. I just don't want you to like me because... I'm a princess." She cast her eyes aside.

My tears stopped flowing, and I wiped them from my cheek. They made my face even colder than it had been before. Another twig snapped in the distance.

This time, I looked past Reina, narrowing my eyes. It was dark out, but I swore I saw a shadowy figure move—a human one. I wished I'd been able to grab the flashlight device Dr. von Breech had demonstrated earlier. But I hadn't. I sidestepped Reina.

"What? I didn't mean to upset you," Reina pleaded.

"Not now." I took off running toward the noise.

I passed through a few trees and ran off the path and into the darker forest area. The sky above had begun misting, the air wetting my face as I ran. The figure I'd seen had attempted to hide rather than run. Once he spotted me, he darted off in earnest, shuffling through the leaves on the ground. I was able to catch up quickly, momentum on my side. I jumped and tackled him, catching him on his legs and forcing him to the ground.

"Oof," the man said.

Reina came up behind me. I pushed myself to my feet. The man in front of me crawled forward. I heard Reina stop in her tracks, and I found myself with the point of a sword at my throat.

"Don't move," a man's voice said. It hadn't been Reina like I'd thought, but another person moving in the forest. This man with a thick, distinct, accent with a bite to it.

Wyranth.

CHAPTER 5

THE REAL REINA CAME UP BEHIND US SHORTLY AFTER THE WYRANTH had ambushed me. She screamed. "James!"

Her presence made my assailant jittery. He poked my neck with the tip of his sword. It stung, but he also was in less of a position to cut my head off than before.

I rolled to the ground, sweeping my foot across and knocking my attacker off balance. The first man got to his feet, and he reached for his sword. I scrambled up, able to draw my blade and deflect his chop at my skull before he could do any damage. Our blades clanged together.

I went on the offensive, understanding that as soon as the second man was able to get to his feet, I'd be at a severe disadvantage. Reina kept yelling behind me, but I couldn't listen to her. I had to focus on my opponent. "Get out of here, Reina. Run!" I shouted without looking back at her.

The Wyranth man was strong, but a little slower than me. I slashed several times at him, forcing him back. I made a quick flurry of strikes and jabbed my blade into his side. The man stumbled, the pain enough to make him drop his blade.

A gunshot rang out behind me.

I turned to see the second man, the one who originally had a blade to my throat, with a pistol pointed at me. "That will be enough resistance, Rislandian," he said.

I didn't have a gun. As an apprentice, I wasn't even supposed to have live steel on me. We were typically relegated to practice blades, but these weren't typical times. Besides, this assignment necessitated that I have some way of defending the princess, so the knights let me keep a blade. I looked forward to becoming a journeyman and obtaining my own, something forged especially for me.

I sure could have used a gun here and now. I chastised myself for not asking for one. Cid would have granted me permission.

The second Wyranth started to shake. "Sir, the little whelp got me good."

The first seemed far more concerned with his companion than me, but still kept his gun trained on me. He moved over to his fellow countryman and helped to hold him up, as the other man was falling. "Geert, you need to be strong. It'll be a ways before we can meet up with our unit."

"I...I..." The man went into convulsions.

I could hardly believe I'd wounded him so severely. I must have penetrated one of his vital organs by accident. The sight was gruesome, and even with having been involved in many battles, I didn't like to watch a wounded man slowly die. It reminded me that my death could be close at hand at any time. I cast my eyes aside.

But I couldn't just sit here and wallow in sympathetic pain for my enemy. I had to do something. Did Reina get out of here and go for help? I wished I had a better way to look and see what she was up to.

The Wyranth growled at me. "You murdered him."

"You're the ones sneaking around in the woods. Why?" I asked.

"We're here to take your king's life and end this farce once and for all."

"So, you're the murderers," I said defiantly. I was trying to keep him talking for as long as I could. If I did, I might have a chance to be rescued by some others.

Unfortunately, it appeared I'd chosen the wrong words.

The Wyranth assassin's arm shook, and he fired his gun at me.

I leaped forward and to the side, prepared to meet my doom. If I was going to die, though, By Malaky I'd take him with me. The first shot missed, but he still held his gun in my direction, and the next one was aimed right for my head. I couldn't change my momentum fast enough to avoid this one.

Something cracked. The Wyranth man stumbled, dropping his compatriot on the ground. He misfired, falling off balance. It gave me an opening to charge him.

I wasted no time, driving my blade right into the Wyranth's chest. It poked out the back and hit the tree behind him. I kicked his gun hand to make sure he wouldn't be able to get another shot off. The gun fell, and when I pulled my blade out, so did the Wyranth.

Something had hit him square in the head. I could see the wound as the assassin's life drained from his eyes in front of me. I didn't look away this time. Even though it was still painful to watch, I felt like I shouldn't leave a man alone in his last moments.

I sheathed my blade and turned to see what had hit him.

Reina stood behind another tree. She had a rock in her hand. "I thought I told you to run."

"I did, just not in the direction you wanted me to," she said.

"You could have been killed."

"Same with you," she said.

"It's my *job* to die for you," I said.

"Maybe I don't want to live without you," Reina said.

The forest fell into an awkward silence. We were right back where we started concerning the conversation, but she'd just escalated her admission of feelings to an absurd degree. A lump grew in my throat. I didn't know what to say. This was all too much, too fast. As much as I was scared, my heart swelled with pride. Reina cared about me. Far more than just for a few fun kisses.

But we couldn't sit here and swoon over each other. There were Wyranth assassins here. They knew the king was here. We had to warn the others. "I still wish you would have listened to me," I said. I picked up the Wyranth's pistol and inspected it. There were still two bullets left in the chamber.

I took a small lap around some trees, pistol facing forward. There didn't appear to be any other Wyranth in our immediate vicinity. "Stay by me," I said. "We should get back and alert the others so we can do a thorough search and make sure there aren't more enemies nearby. It's not safe to be out here alone."

Reina didn't have to be told twice. She linked arms with me. We returned to the path in silence. She shook as we walked. I doubted she'd seen such a bloody scene up close before. Well, she should get used to it. If she were going to be queen one day, she'd deal with far worse than a couple of Wyranth in the woods. If she didn't, well, she'd see a lot worse, too, because it would mean the Wyranth won.

I didn't want to think about the possibility of losing the war, but everywhere we turned there seemed to be yet another villain ready to attack us. When would it end? I found myself glancing at the sky, hoping to see an airship overhead. There was none, just the clouds misting on us, making my face wet and knotting Reina's hair.

I looked to my side, seeing Reina's pale face. She was in shock. I didn't have any words to say to her.

We returned to the lakeside retreat in a few, brief minutes. I was worried about Reina, but I liked having her close by my side. I didn't want to let her go, but we would have to tell the king and the others what happened soon. I doubted King Malaky would like to see Reina dangling on my arm like this. We reached the back porch steps when I saw another shadowy figure moving toward the leftmost wing of the house. No one else was outside when we left.

"Go inside," I said, clutching the Wyranth pistol in my hand.

"James, I'm scared," Reina whispered.

I wiggled my arm away from her death-grip on my bicep. Reina took the hint and made her way up the steps. Even when she was running in fear, she had a graceful movement about her I couldn't help but admire. But I shook my head. I couldn't be staring at her now. There was someone else out there.

I trained my pistol forward and shuffled around the deck area, trying not to make noise with my footsteps. The shadowy figure hadn't been in a hurry. He was moving cautiously. I'd do the same, not alert him with my footsteps.

Reina opened the door and went inside. The door closed behind her with a *thump*.

So much for remaining silent. Hopefully, it wouldn't scare my target too much.

I rounded the corner of the estate, and I stumbled into a taller person standing right in front of me.

"Whoa, don't shoot," the voice said. It was Handley. "What are you doing with a gun anyway?"

"I found it in the forest. There's Wyranth assassins about. What are you doing sneaking around in the shadows?" I said, lowering my pistol to my side.

"Just surveying the perimeter," Handley said. His voice sounded too defensive for my liking. "You should probably go tell King Malaky if there truly are Wyranth spies here."

Was he accusing me of lying? I frowned, not liking his tone in the least. Something about it was wrong. But his words rang true. "Fine," I said, now sounding too defensive myself. I had to be more careful in the way I acted. I wasn't some farm boy anymore. I represented the knights.

"Goodnight," Handley said, continuing on his way around the house.

I turned back for the deck, still fogged by the haze of battle.

CHAPTER 6

"I SWEAR THERE'S SOMETHING UP WITH HANDLEY," I SAID, CLUTCHING A warm cup of tea in between my hands, a blanket draped around me, while I sat in front of the fire next to Reina.

"He told you he was just taking a peek outside, though, didn't he?" Reina asked.

"Yeah," I said. Something didn't sit right with his story. Maybe I'd become a little too paranoid lately, but it seemed like I'd stumbled upon one problem after another in my life as a knight-in-training. I thought back to the night I ran to the top of the Crystal Spire and discovered that Lou, the knight traitor I'd helped bring down months ago, moonlit by informing the Wyranth of Rislandian troop positions.

But not everyone was necessarily a traitor just because I had a bad feeling about them. I didn't like Reggie much, either. He was no traitor, even if he did cheat to get ahead of the other apprentices.

"Don't worry about it too much," Reina said. "What's important is you stopped Wyranth assassins. If they'd gotten into the house, who knows what could have happened?"

I nodded. The reason we waited by the fire was because we needed to brief King Malaky and the others. The king needed time to peel away from further discussions with the Atreblan ambassador, which left Reina and me with more alone time. Even with the comforting warmth of the fire and tea, I couldn't kick my mood of uneasiness. This whole night had been one trauma after another.

The fire crackled, and I stared at it for a long time. How did the world change so rapidly? I thought being a knight would be fun. I'd imagined myself on adventures fighting pirates or dragons or... I don't know what I pictured. But it wasn't standing guard and nearly getting killed by an assassin in the forest. I sighed. "I'm sorry."

Reina blinked, tilting her head at me. "For what?"

"Earlier." Shame from my breakdown over my parents washed over me.

Confusion crossed her face. "I don't know what you're talking about. I'm just happy you found it in your heart to share some of your pains with me. It means we're getting closer."

Did it? I looked into her deep blue eyes. They shone with such hope. She liked me for me. Perhaps the only person in the world other than Zaira who even had a semblance of understanding what being James Gentry meant.

Before I could say anything else, King Malaky and his entourage stalked down the hallway, both Mr. du Gearsmith and Dr. von Breech by his side. The other guards followed.

I set down my teacup and stood before the king, only to bow again.

"At ease, James," King Malaky said, motioning his hand upward. "By all accounts, you've had a hard night and deserve to sit."

I returned to my seat, and King Malaky took a chair across from me. Servants pulled up chairs for the others and, soon, all eyes were on me.

"What happened?" King Malaky asked.

I told him everything to the best of my abilities, leaving out the details of all the personal talk between Reina and me. Our words could remain ours. The king nodded along and frowned when I told him about the Wyranth.

"This is disconcerting," King Malaky said, glancing to the others.

"We need to take extra precautions. It's clear the enemy knows we're here."

"Is there possibly a traitor in our midst giving them information?" Mr. du Gearsmith asked.

The room fell silent.

"I don't want to have to consider that," King Malaky said. "But it's possible." He glanced to the other guards. "Be doubly on the lookout for any of the servants, locals sniffing around, anyone acting suspiciously. I'll also want my guards to scout the forest to make sure we're not dealing with more enemies."

"Yes, Sire," Handley, Tanner, and Reggie said in unison.

Handley shot me a look. I wasn't sure what to make of it, but it froze me. I swallowed. He couldn't think *I* was a traitor, could he? "Shall we go now, your Majesty?" he asked.

"Yes. Let's start the search." King Malaky clasped his hands together. "It's good to hear this story. And James, well done in taking on two Wyranth assassins by yourself. I appreciate you keeping my daughter safe."

"Just doing my duty, Sire," I said. The other knights gathered their belongings. I glanced toward them, wondering if I should be going with them. He called for his guards to go, but I was Reina's.

"Mmm." He glanced between Reina and me. "Oh, and Mr. Gentry, I'd like to talk to you alone, if you wouldn't mind."

The others looked at me as if they didn't envy being in my position. Something in King Malaky's tone let me know this wouldn't be an easy discussion. I was tired after the battle, my adrenaline wearing off to the point where I wanted to collapse in bed, but I couldn't say no to the king. "Of course," I said.

King Malaky stood and motioned for me to follow him.

I lifted myself to my feet. I snuck a glance at Reina, who stared at the fire as if she just wanted to be away from this whole situation. She was in shock from what she'd seen outside. I couldn't blame her. Not everyone had the fortitude to endure some of the horrors I'd seen. I wished she never had to see anything like this again. But I also doubted it would get much more comfortable for her in the coming years, if we survived at all.

The king led me upstairs and into his private chambers. After I stepped through the door, he closed it behind me. "James," he said, his voice low and serious. "You're a good boy. I appreciate your enthusiasm for this kingdom and all you've done these last months."

"Thank you," I said, trying not to come across too timid.

King Malaky sighed and turned to his window, which overlooked the lake. "I dislike interfering in people's lives, including my daughter's. But there's more here than you might understand. Reina is a princess to this kingdom, you understand?"

"I do."

"And, for better or worse, the only heir I will ever have. Her mother succumbed to a cholera epidemic ten years ago."

I'd only been a child at the time, but I recalled my Da coming home with a newspaper, being very upset. My mother crying. They loved the queen. Everyone loved the royal family. But I didn't say anything. I understood his pain, having lost my parents. Would it ever get easier to bear the burden of what I'd lost? The thought made me frown.

"As such, she has certain duties and obligations that necessitate her forgoing a normal life. She has a lot to learn...in case something happens to me, or if only for the future."

"I know," I said.

King Malaky turned back to face me. "I dislike disappointing my subjects, but you are my subjects all the same. James, we're in negotiations with the Atreblans, and even though McRose speaks as if marriage to the prince is but a trifle, she cares about that more than she lets on. And if we can get the Atreblans away from demanding airship technology..."

I'd already been thinking about all of this, but hearing it from King Malaky made it hurt a lot more than I would have expected. It was as if the Wyranth assassin had stabbed me in the gut. I felt like I was bleeding out in front of him. I couldn't lose Reina, not like this. "But what about..." I found myself questioning the king. Was I this much of an idiot? I shut my mouth.

"What about what?" King Malaky asked.

"Nothing, Sire," I said.

"You have my permission to speak freely."

I searched his eyes, and they appeared earnest. For all the pomp and ritual that surrounded meeting King Malaky the first time, he seemed like he didn't want any part of such things. He was such a normal person. How did he ever end up King of Rislandia? "What about being your only heir? If she goes to Atrebla, wouldn't the kingdom lose an heir?"

"We were thinking of arranging it so the Atreblan prince would come here and join her as a Rislandian. Since he's not the heir to the throne, it would make sense for both of our kingdoms."

"Oh," I said, my shoulders slumping. I hadn't considered that.

"But for now, we would send Reina to Atrebla, if only to maintain her own protection in the middle of this war."

This was going far worse than I wanted. I was going to lose Reina both in the near and long-term. It wasn't fair! I'd done everything I was supposed to. I wanted to beg King Malaky, plead with him to reconsider, but I couldn't do it. He was my king, and he did what was best for the kingdom. In other circumstances, he might have allowed Reina to do whatever she chose. Her life would be her own. But these were the worst of all possible times. The Wyranth were everywhere we turned, and they weren't going to let up soon.

It didn't make his words sting any less, though. This was the worst night of my life.

"She'll get to know the prince there. I won't force her into a marriage, but she'll understand her duty and what it means. It's my hope they'll get along, at the very least," King Malaky said.

He didn't need to justify it to me. I understood. The good of the kingdom. Everything I did was for that good, and I'd continue to. Even if it meant losing everything. It's what being a knight was all about.

"What I'm trying to say is, I know the two of you have become close." He held up a hand. "I don't want to know how close. A father doesn't need details. But I want you to understand the political situation here. This plan could be a matter of Rislandia's survival. I like you, James, but I can't have you getting in the way of that."

I wanted to burst into tears. Again.

Dread spun in my gut, making me topsy-turvy. All I could think about was burying my head in a pillow and ignoring the world. Maybe forever. But I couldn't let the king see me as weak or unreliable. I bit on my lower lip hard to keep it from quivering. I would hold steady, even through this. "Yes, Sire," I managed to say.

"Thank you for understanding, James. You're an amazing knight. You're going to go places. I appreciate you being able to talk to me like this, man to man."

I nodded. He had no idea how hard it was to keep myself from completely falling apart.

"You're dismissed."

I bowed and turned from him. Fortunately, I managed to hold my tears until after pushing my way out the door.

CHAPTER 7

DESPITE BEING INCREDIBLY TIRED, I FOUND MYSELF UNABLE TO SLEEP. My mind whirled, even as my body ached and whined, but there was little I could do. All I could think about was Reina. I shouldn't think about her. I couldn't have her. King Malaky had made it clear. How could I defy my king?

But I loved her. I cared far more about her than just stealing kisses. I'd follow Reina anywhere, do anything for her. Beyond my duty as her guard, I would die for her.

The king telling me, in essence, to leave his daughter alone only solidified that which I'd been trying to figure out for so long. There was nothing I wouldn't do for Reina, including leaving her alone if I needed to. By Malaky, why did my chest hurt so badly when I had to think about it?

My tossing and turning annoyed Reggie. He threw his pillow at me. "We need to sleep, Gentry," he muttered. "We already spent too much energy tonight rummaging through the forest."

"I can't," I said. It wasn't my intention. There was nothing I wanted to do other than sleep, and maybe not wake up again. I hated everything. But it wasn't Reggie's fault, as much as I wanted to bite his head off just for being there.

I tossed the pillow back to him, and Reggie promptly put it over his head, turning his body away from me.

Sleep still wouldn't come, however. After several more minutes of moping, I decided it would be best if I got up and did something —*anything*. I slid my legs over the side of my bed, my body so weary it protested each and every movement. After a few breaths of making sure I wanted to get up, I stood and slipped my boots on.

I'd go for a walk. At the very least, I could get my thoughts out, make myself more tired, and then if all went well, I'd finally be able to sleep. It seemed like a better idea than lying there bothering Reggie.

I tread carefully as I made my way out of the room, trying not to make the floorboards creak and wake Reggie or any of the others. There would be a couple of guards on night watch at the king's retreat. I hoped I wouldn't bother them, either.

I just wanted to think and to be alone. Maybe not alone. In truth, I hoped Reina would have a similar lack-of-sleeping problem and have the same idea I did.

She wasn't in the front room when I arrived. The gas lights were out, and the fire in the hearth had turned to nothing but smoldering embers. It still radiated heat. I placed my hands in front of the fire and rubbed them together.

Then I looked at the door.

It would be freezing outside at this time of night, but what did I care? The cold would shake me and do me some good.

I stepped to the door and opened it. The chill hit my face and coat-less body immediately. It was quite the jolt to the system, but it didn't faze me. I'd already endured so much cold this evening in other ways, what could a little weather do to me?

I slipped through the threshold and closed the door behind me. Despite my brave thoughts, I stuck my hands in my pockets. It would be so nice if Reina were out here with me right now, her hands on my arm, pressed against my side, awkwardly walking and bumping into each other. I longed to return to those moments before I had spotted the Wyranth assassins.

I sighed, causing my breath to mist in front of me. Reina wouldn't be coming out here, no matter how hard I willed it. It wasn't as if she could sense my thoughts, and there was no way I was going to go to her room and try to wake her after King Malaky's talk. It would probably get me thrown out of the compound. Then I'd be even further away from her.

But if she had to go to Atrebla, would I ever be close with her again? Maybe it would be worth the risk to get to spend one more night with her.

I clenched my fists in my pockets, grabbing ahold of the pant fabric. I wanted to rip it. I wanted to punch someone. I just wanted this feeling to go away so I could go back to working on becoming the greatest knight Rislandia had ever produced.

I shuffled forward, dragging my feet across the deck as I moved. Soon enough, I found myself at the base of the forest path we'd walked earlier. It dawned on me that it could be dangerous out here, even though the other knights hadn't found any sign of more Wyranth earlier. This time, I didn't bring my sword belt or my newfound pistol, which no one had bothered to take away from me yet. A foolish move. I knew better. But I also didn't care.

If there were more Wyranth out here, well, then, they could kill me. Or I'd tear them apart with my bare hands. They wouldn't want to mess with me right now.

The thought brought an angry smile to my face as I walked. I picked up my pace, jogging, and then I burst into a full run. It felt great to run. The wind bit my face with its cold, but I was alive. Doing something felt much better than doing nothing. Part of me wanted to keep going down this path, disappear around the lake, into the Oler Mountains, and never come back.

But I couldn't do that. I had my duties. I would never renege on those, no matter what. My personal feelings be damned.

I didn't know how long I'd been running for, but it was a while and, finally, my lungs started to burn. The cold disappeared into my overheated body. Sweat beaded under my clothing. I was out of breath. I slowed to a stop and put my hands on my hips to regain some of my composure.

And for the second time this evening, I saw someone else. In the dark with the clouds, it was just a silhouette moving, but this one walked toward me from a distance.

In this shape, there'd be no way I could confront an enemy. So I ducked into the forest, away from the path. A couple of trees concealed me. Hopefully, the other person hadn't spotted me on the trail.

I stayed quiet, remaining still as best I could. The figure came down the path, edging closer. It was a man, and he didn't bother concealing his steps, likely not thinking anyone else was out here. At least, I hoped he didn't know anyone else was out here.

The man finally reached where I'd been on the path, and he gave pause. He turned in my direction, facing the tree I used as my cover.

Uh oh.

"I see you there," a voice said. A *shkk* sounded, the unmistakable sound of a man drawing a sword. "Come out."

I considered the gruff voice, recognizing it. Handley! Again. I stepped out of the trees.

"Gentry?" Handley asked in an incredulous tone. He sheathed his sword. "What are you doing out here?"

"Trying to think, get away for a bit so I can sleep," I said. "You?"

"Same."

I stepped toward the path and saw Handley in earnest. He looked none too happy to see me there. Something was up with him, that much was clear. But what if he was having some personal problems like I was? I didn't want to accuse him of wrongdoing when I was guilty of much the same actions he was.

"Let's head back. You're pretty far out for this time of night, especially considering that you stumbled upon Wyranth earlier tonight." He didn't wait but moved down the path.

I followed him, saying nothing, tucking my hands back into my pockets. I didn't want to be around another person. The whole point was to go out alone—or with Reina if she happened to be around. I scanned the periphery, hopeful, even though I knew there was no way she'd appear.

"A little advice," Handley said as he walked. "You're going to get yourself into trouble. You're snooping around constantly, going off where you shouldn't be. That's not what we're here to do. Just stick by the princess and stop worrying so much."

I grunted my assent, hoping it would be enough.

"What's worrying you, anyway?"

"I don't want to talk about it," I said. How could I tell him that the princess *was* what worried me? Maybe he knew I'd been quietly courting her. We hadn't done much to hide our affections. Either way, I didn't want to air my feelings to him.

"Fine," he said.

We walked in idle silence for a long time, before I couldn't handle it anymore. I needed to say something to make the mood less awkward. "I wish I had some way to communicate with Zaira about the Wyranth here. She'd probably appreciate some information on their movements."

Handly scoffed. "The important people for such knowledge are here. The von Monocles do little for the kingdom. They're just a show."

I clenched my fist. "They're good people. Zaira's like a sister to me." Hopefully, my warning would stop him from saying anything worse about Zair-bear.

Handley's face tightened as if he were holding back anger. "I had a real sister once."

"What happened?"

"I don't want to talk about it," he said.

We returned to our awkward silence. So much for a peaceful outing to help me sleep. It gave me an uneasy feeling to be around Handley, especially with him getting so angry over a simple conversation. He remained quiet as he opened the door to the estate and motioned me inside.

I was left with even more to worry about.

CHAPTER 8

STANDING GUARD AFTER A DAY OF HARD BATTLE AND A NIGHT WHERE I couldn't sleep at all proved very difficult. I wanted to lean to one side or rub my eyes, or just lie down and rest, but I had my duty. It wasn't like this was the worst thing in my life I'd endured, even if it had crushed my heart and my spirit far more than any other of the trials I'd faced. I tried not to look at Reina, even though the crimson dress she wore today made her look even more stunning than usual.

Mr. du Gearsmith arrived with the Atreblans, introducing them formally. Bows and handshakes were exchanged between King Malaky and Ambassador McRose. Everyone else waited and seated themselves after the two leaders settled into their chairs. Dr. von Breech sat at the king's side, his arm resting on the box of his contraptions he'd shown us the other day. From what I'd overheard of King Malaky practicing his pitch to the Atreblans earlier in the morning, they intended to work out a trade for these basic technologies in exchange for Atreblan military support. Everyone seemed so nervous. Did the fate of the kingdom depend on this meeting?

I wished I could have been more enthusiastic about the proceedings, but I was so tired. As McRose and King Malaky began their ritualistic small talk, my eyelids became so heavy I could hardly keep them open. I dozed off where I stood for a few moments before Tanner nudged me in the side to bring me back to alertness. Fortunately, I didn't make any noise or snore. None of the dignitaries seemed to notice.

I'd missed Dr. von Breech opening the crate of goods, holding out the flashlight and displaying it for Ambassador McRose. She looked very impressed with the light. "And you say the arm contraption is a weapon that shoots electricity?"

Dr. von Breech nodded. "It does. You reverse-engineer and fabricate a few hundred of these, and you'll find yourself with far less of a problem with your goblins in the north. You might even eradicate it completely."

King Malaky inclined his head as if it would be an excellent idea.

McRose brought a finger to her lips, her eyes scanning Dr. von Breech's inventions. "These would be life changing for our soldiers, and even our civilians, but King Eakin didn't send me here to peruse Rislandia's latest in engineering." She brought her hand down and sighed. "I'm afraid we still are at an impasse."

"Even with Reina returning to court with you?" King Malaky asked.

Reina's face tightened considerably. Most other people might not have noticed it, but I could tell she was very uncomfortable with the idea. I wanted to shout against her leaving, but after King Malaky spoke to me yesterday, how could I? It wasn't my place to interfere with the king's negotiations, no matter the pain it caused my heart.

McRose shook her head, which caused me great relief. Did this mean Reina wouldn't have to go away? I could only hope it would be the case. "I'm sorry, King Malaky, and your assorted guests. I'm afraid I was sent here with one mission, and if it's not something on the table, I should return to my kingdom and let them know Rislandia is still unwilling to share in their travel technology. It's a good thing your kingdom's in a position to refuse aid." She stood.

"You know that's not fair," King Malaky said, standing right along with her. "Please, sit down. Have some refreshments. There has to be some way to work this out to our mutual advantage."

"I wish the circumstances were different. Your daughter is quite lovely, as have been your accommodations. I will certainly let King Eakin know of your hospitality."

Mr. du Gearsmith moved to cut her off. "Sheila, for me...for my people," he pleaded.

Her eyes went a little wide at the sudden move, and her lips pursed. It caused her a moment's pause, but she turned her head to the side. "I'm sorry. This isn't a personal affair. I have orders from my kingdom. My abilities to negotiate are limited." She tightened her face with a firm resolve and snapped her fingers. "Guards, help me retrieve my things. Perhaps if you change your mind while I'm packing, I might be able to return to King Eakin with better news."

McRose and her entourage left the room, leaving a stunned Rislandian delegation.

Everyone looked so hopeless. I was trying to hide my delight. I wouldn't lose Reina after all. She wouldn't be going with them. It was like all of the panic of the last day evaporated before my eyes. I felt so light I could float.

And I felt terrible about it.

Everyone was so down. King Malaky had sunk back into his chair, his face in his hands. The others consoled him. We were about to lose our kingdom, and I was gleeful about a girl.

Great going, I thought. Even though no one else could sense my thoughts, I had to deal with my own inner-treason that I would choose Reina over the kingdom.

"I don't know what to do," King Malaky said.

"We can't give the airship technology. We are the only ones in the world with such a capability. We have to maintain our advantage as long as we possibly can," Mr. du Gearsmith said.

King Malaky looked up. "Even if we don't exist?"

"We will have to trust in the von Monocles to do their magic. We've always said their luck is extraordinary, and it's worked for us so far," Mr. du Gearsmith said, standing and smoothing down his coat.

"I don't want the kingdom to have to rely on superstition for its survival," King Malaky said. He stood, and so did the others. "But we're not desperate enough to give up our airships just yet. Reina, join me in my quarters. We have planning to do." He tried to appear as resolved as possible before us—a frowning face, stoic—but I could see in his eyes he was shaken. His attention briefly drifted toward me before he made way for the stairs.

Reina gave me a weak smile as she passed.

"Well, then. I'd better tell Ambassador McRose she'll indeed be returning to Atrebla empty-handed," Mr. du Gearsmith said. He bowed his head toward us guards. "Enjoy this break while you can. I have a feeling it won't last long."

CHAPTER 9

KING MALAKY AND REINA SPENT THE REST OF THE DAY ALONE. WHAT they discussed, I had no idea. I was able to coax the other guards into allowing me to nap until Reina came back down the stairs. For once, Reggie had a little compassion for me. "You kept me up all night so you must be tired, but you owe me one," he said.

I slept until he came to wake me, which was when the king and princess came down for dinner. They requested a private dinner with Mr. du Gearsmith and Dr. von Breech. The guards and the staff weren't invited this time. We ate alone, out in the main room.

The atmosphere in the house had gone from nervous to dismal. No one wanted to so much as say a word to each other. I was afraid of saying something wrong and making someone snap. How had we come to this place?

I prodded my roasted meat with my fork, finding myself not hungry. How could I eat when we were on the cusp of losing everything we'd fought so hard for? My stomach knotted, much like it had when I was faced with the prospect of losing Reina.

But now I wouldn't lose her, right? We could be together? It hadn't felt like it these last few hours.

One of the servants slid open the accordion doors, and Reina emerged from the dining room. She looked as radiant as ever, but her face seemed paler, some of the sparkle lost from her eyes. Was it from the stress of planning battles with the king, or from having come face to face with the gore of battle yesterday?

She stepped delicately toward us in the main room. Even when distraught, it was as if she floated on the air rather than walked like the rest of us. My heart pounded as I watched her.

"I think I'll take another step outside," Reina announced.

"After what happened last night?" King Malaky asked, trailing behind her.

"I won't go far this time, just to the deck. Besides, James will be with me. There won't be a problem." She spun her head around as if to taunt her father with me.

King Malaky frowned. At this rate, I wouldn't last very long as a guard. The king would kill me before the Wyranth ever could. What was she thinking? "Fine. James, I want you to take the auto-electro-cuter with you this time. Just in case. It'll give you an edge if there are more problems."

I wanted to jump for joy, but I contained myself. I had to look professional and not like a wide-eyed young farm boy excited to play with the new weapons. Finally, people trusted me with the gadgets the knights were known for. "Yes, your Majesty," I said, trying to contain my glee. I gave one of the servants my plate and dug into Dr. von Breech's box to grab the device.

Dr. von Breech rushed over to assist me with it as if it were something easy to break. He clasped it on my right arm. "You remember how to use it?"

"I do," I said.

"And you won't unless it's absolutely necessary? I don't want any problems, especially with the wooden deck out back. It could catch fire easily if this was misfired."

"Got it," I said. The device weighed heavy on my arm, but with the power I wielded as I bent it toward me, I'd carry something ten times the weight anytime.

Reina proceeded outside. I gave my bows to my betters and

hurried after her. Her breath created vapor around her, and she crossed her arms from the cold. It seemed chillier tonight than it had the prior evening.

I closed the door and jogged to catch up with her. She leaned over the railing of the deck. I mirrored her movements.

"Do you ever feel like there's no point? Like nothing you do is ever going to be worthwhile or good enough?" Reina asked.

I bit my lip. "Yeah. All the time."

She let out a small laugh that sounded more sad than humorous. "If you feel that way, there's no hope for the rest of us."

"What do you mean? I'm just a farm boy who's thrown into the strange world of politics and monsters."

"But which is the politician and which is the monster?" Reina turned toward me.

I cocked a brow at her. "Is there something you want to tell me?"

Reina smacked me in the chest. "I open up to you, and you call me a monster? Really." She pouted, her lip jutting out.

I took the opportunity to press my face against hers and kiss her. Even though it ended up being a quick peck, I found myself tingling at the touch of her soft lips.

She stumbled backward and laughed in earnest this time. "You scared me, moving like that."

"Yeah, but you liked it."

"I did," Reina said. Her paleness went away, her cheeks flushing.

"I thought I was going to lose you," I said, unable to keep my feelings under control any longer. It was as if the kiss made it all pour out of me. I'd been staring at her for over a day, wanting to tell her everything. The good in me, the bad. Everything I loved, everything I hated. I wanted to lay it all out as a sacrifice to her in hopes it would please her.

"I wouldn't let that happen," she said quietly. She studied me.

I gripped the rail, afraid I'd lose my balance from being so weak-kneed. "Your father, though…"

"He talked to you," Reina said, searching.

I nodded.

"And told you I was going to go off with some Atreblan prince, no doubt." She wrinkled her nose and turned toward the lake.

"Yeah," I said.

"I wish he hadn't done that. It's my decision, my life. I'll do what I have to save the kingdom, but he should know better. I should go talk to him."

"I'd rather you stay here," I said.

Reina glanced at me.

I offered my hand.

She took it.

I looked up at the stars. "You know, this reminds me of the first time my Da took me hunting in the forests north of Plainsroad Village..."

We stayed there, holding hands, talking about our childhoods for what must have been hours. The moon peeked through the clouds in the sky, no rain or misting tonight. At least for now. It shone on the lake, a tiny, bending ray of light like it was reaching out for us. My shoulders relaxed. With Reina beside me, I could do anything. She seemed to enjoy being with me as much as I did with her. The way she laughed, teased.

The conversation lulled. She leaned in toward me. I took the opportunity for another kiss, and I wouldn't settle for a peck this time. Our lips touched softly, and hers parted. The heat of her mouth locked with mine in the cold night air was like heaven. Her tongue grazed mine, a light touch, everything I ever wanted not, just from a woman, but from life. Warmth filled me.

I wrapped my arm around her, careful not to set off the auto-electrocuter by mistake, and pulled her body against me. Even through the leathers of my knight's attire, I could feel both the softness and firmness of her slender frame. I wanted nothing more than to stay in this moment forever.

Eventually, we had to break the kiss. She kept her eyes closed as she pulled back, a broad smile across her face. I wished I had a photograph of her expression, but I wouldn't likely forget it all the same. I would keep it locked inside my memories. I stifled a breath, unable to help but be in awe of her beauty.

"It's late," she said, opening her eyes. She followed with a yawn.

"Yeah, it is," I said.

"I'm going to head back inside," Reina said. She motioned me to join her.

"If you don't mind, I'd like to stay here awhile. I took a long nap earlier, and I'm not so tired."

Reina brushed the back of her fingers against my cheek. "Don't stay out too late," she said.

"I won't."

She turned and sauntered back to the door. It might have been my imagination, but it seemed like her hips swayed a little more when she walked. Was she teasing me? If she was, I wanted more of it.

I sighed when she closed the door and gazed out upon the lake. How crazy was this? My moods could shift from despair to pure elation within hours, and all because of what one girl said or did. It was dangerous to have someone else hold so much power over me, but I didn't care. She could have it all.

Something moved off to my left. I narrowed my eyes. It had to be Handley again. Why did he bother me so much? Thinking of him made me stop thinking of Reina, and that brought up a fire in me. I'd let him have it. He wouldn't lecture me this time.

I stomped across the deck over to the other side of the residence and turned the corner. There, I saw Handley as I'd suspected, but not where I'd expected to find him. He was dangling from a rope, propelling himself up the wall, into the house.

"Handley?" I asked.

He looked down at me. He had one leg through a window. He didn't seem to want to stop. What was he doing out here? He disappeared into the room.

I frowned, considering what I'd just seen, trying to figure out where in the house he'd just gone. The roof wasn't very accessible from the ground. Handley's securing a rope up there had to have taken him some doing. My eyes widened as I realized the only place he could have been heading—the king's bedroom!

CHAPTER 10

I BOLTED TOWARD THE DOOR. THE MIST AND DEW ON THE DECK MADE me slip, and I skidded the rest of the way to the wall before using it to right myself. I was lucky I didn't fall through the glass and shatter it.

I slid the door open, pushing it behind me but not seeing if I shut it all the way.

Reina caught sight of me rushing through the open room. Shock crossed her face like she couldn't tell whether to chastise me or be concerned.

"No time!" I said, bushing by her. An inch to my left and I might have run her over. I propelled myself up the stairs, not wasting a moment on whatever she might have said.

I hurried down the hall and gripped the king's bedroom door handle. It wouldn't turn. I fudged with it several times, but it wouldn't give. It had to be locked.

Voices stirred at the commotion I'd caused, but there wasn't time to deliberate. I lowered my shoulder and rammed the door with the full weight of my body.

If this had been the oversized, thick doors of the Rislandia City palace, I would have bounced back with a bruised shoulder, or worse, but in this estate, the doors were thinner. The wood cracked around the hinges, but it didn't budge all the way. I wondered—would the auto-electrocuter be able to break down the door? I held my hand up to it.

Crack.

It wasn't the auto-electrocuter making the noise—but a gunshot! I hadn't depressed the lever. By Malaky, I hoped I wasn't too late.

I depressed the lever on my gadget. Electricity shot from it, sending a wave of energy toward the door. The lock snapped, sending the door swinging inward. I hurried forward, but lost my balance and fell face-first on the ground.

When I looked up, I saw Handley with a smoking pistol in his hand. He'd fired at King Malaky's bed. He looked none too pleased to see me there. "I told you to mind your own business, James!"

I scrambled to my feet. Handley pointed the weapon at me. I glanced out of the corner of my eye, more concerned about the well-being of King Malaky than the man in front of me. If the king had been hit...

Feathers floated in the air where the king's head should have rested, a bullet hole blasted through the pillow, but King Malaky wasn't on his bed. He had rolled behind it and now crept up to get a view of both Handley and me.

My jumbling with the door must have alerted him before Handley could get his shot off.

I pulled the lever of the auto-electrocuter. Nothing came out this time. It rumbled, as if it were charging. I hoped it needed to charge and wasn't out of aether-fuel.

This was bad. I was in close quarters and didn't know how I'd be able to fight off a journeyman like Handley on my own. If I could only stall long enough to get the other guards here...

Unless they were in on it, too. What if I was the only one loyal to the king? If I couldn't trust Handley, could I trust anyone?

"Why?" I asked Handley.

Before he could answer, a voice came from downstairs. "James? Father? Is everything okay?" Reina.

Handley kept his gun trained on me, but spoke to the king. "Tell her everything is fine and you don't want to see any of the guards. You want to talk with James alone. Or I swear I'm going to shoot him through the skull and you next."

King Malaky gulped, looking torn as he righted himself. "I'm fine, Reina," he said, though his voice quivered. "I want to talk with James alone for a moment. Don't let anyone come up here."

"Very good," Handley said.

I shot a glance at King Malaky. Didn't he know Handley would kill us no matter what? We were in an impossible situation now, with the auto-electorcuter out of commission.

It made sense why Handley had been sneaking around outside. He'd been scoping out the area, trying to find a way inside. With King Malaky locking his door at night, he wouldn't be able to get in the usual way without causing too much of a commotion. As a knight himself, he probably relieved the night guards and set up a situation where he'd be alone with the king. It would have worked perfectly, if I hadn't happened to be outside kissing the princess.

"You want to know why, James?" Handley sneered. "For the good of the kingdom. Rislandia is weak under Malaky's leadership. It's his fault the Wyranth are invading our borders. His fault my sister..." he trailed off, his hand starting to shake as he turned his head to the side. "It's best you don't know the details. What's important is a change in leadership. It's the only way."

"And who's going to lead? Reina?"

Handley grimaced. He hadn't thought this through. He was acting out of rage for whatever happened to his sister. I knew his pain so well. I'd buried it deep inside me when my parents died. But I didn't blame King Malaky. The king did everything he could to be fair to his subjects and keep us safe without stepping on our lives. It wasn't his fault the Wyranth had their bizarre soldier serum fueling their crazed war. But I knew arguing with him would do no good.

"You don't have to do this," I said.

"I've made my choice. You'll thank me for it. Just back away and pretend you didn't see this."

"You know I can't do that," I said, reaching for my sword.

Handley fired a shot. It hit my sword perfectly. The hilt clanged against my hip when the bullet ricocheted off it. He could have blown off my leg! I was lucky I had the sword there and that his shot had struck so true, even as the pain began to flare from the sheer force of the impact. I shifted my weight to my other leg, trying to keep focused.

"Fight me like a man," I said.

King Malaky crept behind Handley. If could stall him a few more seconds, the king might overpower him.

"I only have a little bit of time. We both know that," Handley said. He spun as if knowing exactly where the king had positioned himself. He pressed the barrel of the pistol upward against King Malaky's chin. "I'm sorry I had to do this, your Majesty, but you can't keep letting this kingdom get smashed into bits to protect the von Monocles and their blasted airship."

"It's not about them," King Malaky said.

"It's always about them!" Handley spat.

I had to do something. But what? One shot from Handley would end King Malaky's life. If the auto-electrocuter had regained its charge, the king was too close for me to safely fire it. I was stuck.

King Malaky took the initiative for me. He stomped his foot onto Handley's toe, causing the man to recoil backward. The move surprised the traitorous knight, and he lost his position, stumbling back. He pulled the trigger, and a shot resounded.

CHAPTER 11

KING MALAKY TOOK A BULLET. BLOOD SPLATTERED FROM THE WOUND. I couldn't turn away, more afraid than I'd ever been. King Malaky had always been larger than life to me. He was the king! He couldn't *bleed*.

Handley stumbled back, allowing me to get a better look at the king. He clutched his shoulder. He'd been shot in the shoulder, not the head! He might have a chance at living yet.

But I had to act. With Handley's gun now pointed away from King Malaky, I drew my sword. It took much more effort with the heavy auto-electrocuter on my arm, but I still didn't dare use the experimental device within such proximity to King Malaky.

I pushed forward, hollering to try to distract Handley.

The journeyman knight had the wherewithal to drop his pistol and grab his own sword in close quarters. He barely drew in time to deflect my strike. For now, I had the advantage. He had his back close to a wall, and I had the whole space of the room to work with, as long as King Malaky didn't get in the way.

I struck hard and true, but Handley had the upper hand in speed. He stopped my second blow, and my third. Even though I was firmly on the attack, I couldn't get past his defenses.

King Malaky fell between us. He collapsed to the ground with his full weight, pushing my sword to the side, and fortunately only hitting its flat. My sword *clanked* against the wall.

Handley took the opportunity to become the aggressor. He hopped over the fallen king, driving a blow at me. I lifted my sword to hold it off and kicked him when he landed close to me. My foot connected with his gut and sent him stumbling back again. His footwork was nimble enough to miss tripping over the king.

He laughed. "You're good, James Gentry. But I'm out of time," he said, darting for the window.

I wouldn't let him get away. I hopped over King Malaky, but I landed where his blood began to pool. The blood was slick and made me lose my footing, just as the moist deck had done outside. I went tumbling into the wall.

Handley scrambled through the open window by the time I recovered. I jabbed with my sword, narrowly missing his foot as he passed through.

"The king is down!" I shouted. "He's hurt and needs healing!" Hopefully, someone would hear me. I couldn't let Handley get away with this. If King Malaky died…

I didn't want to think about the consequences. It was on me to stop him from getting away. I pivoted and dove out the window onto the angled rooftop.

Handley was already getting onto his rope. I wished I would have doubled back earlier when I noticed him lurking around this side of the house and looked for irregularities. Next time, I would remember.

I carefully turned around and slid on my rear down the shingles of the roof until I reached the top of the rope. Then I grabbed ahold of it and leaped off it. Handley was near the bottom. I let myself slide down the rope quickly. The momentum burned my hands, bringing heat and a stinging sensation I would regret later, but I had to hurry. Halfway down, I let go and dropped, landing atop Handley's shoulders.

The sudden weight caused Handley to tumble the rest of the way to the ground. "I've had about enough of you!" he growled as we struggled, entangled together on the grass.

He socked me in the ribs with a punch. It hurt, but I didn't hear anything crack. I tried to push him off me, but he was bigger and heavier, not to mention more muscular. He threw more punches, and I absorbed them, unable to move, as he had me stuck to the ground.

I still had one trick up my sleeve—the sleeve itself. I'd hesitated to use it earlier, but now that there weren't any bystanders close to us, the auto-electrocuter became an option. I'd wanted to capture Handley. If he was part of some bigger plot, we could have used the information. It had sounded like he acted alone, but it never hurt to double check.

Handley delivered a hard blow to my face, punishing me for my moment of indecision. His knuckles hit my cheekbone and rattled my whole skull. When it connected, it was like someone shined lights directly in my eyes. I felt like I was swimming in a deep pond. And then pain flared in my face. I wanted to cradle the wound, but I couldn't.

I tried to wiggle free, managing at least to get my arms loose enough to block his next punch. He was trying to kill me. I couldn't hold back any longer.

I aimed my arm at Handley and made a fist. My fingers depressed the lever, and the device whirred.

Handley's eyes widened in fear and shock as he noticed the band around my arm.

Electricity burst from the device, steam shooting back into my face. It was hot and burned the already painful wound I'd suffered from Handley's last punch. More bright light filled my vision, but it wasn't inside my head this time. The light filled Handley, and he convulsed uncontrollably. His eyes rolled back, and his jaw went slack. He made a grunting noise.

I averted my eyes.

Despite him being a traitor, I didn't enjoy seeing a fellow knight fried to a crisp. Despite looking away, I couldn't get away from the horror of his death. His flesh smelled like charred meat. Smoke rose from him and blew in my face.

Finally, his body went limp, and he fell to the side. I released the firing mechanism and took the opportunity to roll out from under him. His body was charred alright, all of his hair and clothes singed. It looked like a terrifying way to die, but I was just thankful to have made it out alive. I pushed myself to a knee and took several gulps of air to catch my breath.

Reina came running from the estate, along with the other guards. They stopped before the scene, eyes darting between Handley and me in confusion. "What happened?" Reina asked. "Was he working for the Wyranth?"

I swallowed, my throat dry after expending myself. "I think he was acting on his own. I'll tell you about it later. Your father?"

She frowned. "His personal doctor is attending him. He's lost a lot of blood."

I'd gotten there too late. If only I'd moved a little faster, or found out Handley's scheme earlier. I cursed myself silently as the other knights came to help me to my feet.

EPILOGUE

I spent the night pacing the main room. Even though my body dragged from so little rest these last few days, I found for yet another evening, I couldn't sleep. I worried too much if King Malaky would make it out alive. I wasn't the only one with insomnia.

We'd done about all the patrols we could do. It didn't appear as if there were more Wyranth at the king's retreat beyond the two we'd found scouting the woods. We were safe from the invasion for now.

Everyone gathered in the main room. No one talked. We all needed to be there for each other, but what could we say?

Hours passed. The servants brought us tea and more of the coffee Tanner found so enticing. I happily accepted a cup, even though I didn't like the taste. It helped me stay alert.

Something *creaked* on the staircase, and I turned. King Malaky's doctor came down the stairs. He had a receding hairline with white hair, a matching beard, and round spectacles. His name was Dr. Bruce, and he was a calm and soft-spoken man. He looked as weary as we were.

Did his expression mean King Malaky didn't make it? I turned my head toward Reina.

She stood from her seat at the fire. "Is he...?"

Dr. Bruce clasped his hands together. "He's awake. Finally. He's very weak, though. I wouldn't recommend everyone rush in at once."

Reina started forward. "I'll talk to him."

Dr. Bruce held up a finger. "Actually, he requested to speak with Mr. Gentry first, if it would be all right by your highness."

Reina's mouth went agape. She wasn't used to being second fiddle in anything. "Why..." she cleared her throat. "Of course. Whatever my father wishes."

I blinked. What could he possibly want with me? Reina's face searched me as if she were just as confused as I was, but I couldn't exactly say no. "Right," I said and turned toward the stairs.

Dr. Bruce made way for me, and I found myself in front of the king's bedroom. The door was still busted in from my work earlier in the evening. It was cracked open enough for King Malaky to spot me from his bed. He shifted a little when he noticed me but didn't give any other indication that he'd seen me.

I stepped inside, careful in my movements. I didn't want to spook him or inadvertently injure him more. King Malaky's face shone with sweat. He had deep bags under his eyes and didn't look recovered at all.

"Your Majesty," I said.

"Come closer," King Malaky said, his voice no more than a croak of a whisper.

I shuffled over to his bedside and took a knee beside him. His breath was heavy and foul from lying there and just waking up. I wouldn't flinch, though. He was the king. I had to act like all was right.

"I wanted to thank you for tonight. Without you, I wouldn't be here," he said.

"Just doing my duty, Sire," I said.

"It was more than that. No one else in the house noticed anything wrong. You were vigilant, and you put your life on the line to protect me. And you succeeded. I'm alive." He paused, panting.

Would he be for long? I didn't want to exacerbate him. I didn't know what to say, so I kept my lips shut tight.

"Your dedication made me think about a lot of things. What we're fighting for in Rislandia, the importance of it all beyond just my health. Reina is the future, whether she becomes queen sooner or later. You're the future, as well. I shouldn't be jeopardizing her, or you, for short-term treaties in this war, any more than I should give out the airship technology. You're the heart and soul of Rislandia."

I inclined my head proudly. I never thought I'd hear the king shower me in such praise. It felt amazing, pure validation for these last few days of struggle. I couldn't have asked for more.

"As such, I want to reward you rightly. And the reason I call you in now...if there are complications later, I want you to know." He coughed and groaned, vast amounts of pain showing on his face. "Would you mind summoning Reina? I'm afraid my voice won't carry."

"Reina!" I shouted.

King Malaky winced at the volume of my voice. I gave him a sheepish smile, but he'd asked for it.

Reina sauntered through the open door soon after. "Is everything okay?" she asked, her eyes scanning. Those beautiful blue orbs fell upon King Malaky, and she rushed over to him. "Father!"

"I'm alive, my dear," King Malaky said.

Tears fell down her cheeks. "I was so worried."

"Don't fret for me. I've had a good life. I still hope to." He chuckled but stopped himself mid-laugh as the pain caught up with him. "I wanted to talk to both of you. I know you've been...less than discreet with your relationship."

"I can explain," I started, bumbling over myself. Had he watched us kissing earlier in the evening? He didn't have a window that faced the lake. We'd been so stupid.

"It's not James's fault," Reina said. She crossed her arms over her chest.

"The young are so quick to react, to get defensive," King Malaky said. He sighed. "No, I don't mean to chastise you over your love. Nearly dying has brought me a new perspective. I want to encourage you, Reina. James is a loyal, hard-working man, and I want to give my blessing for him to court you."

My jaw dropped. Was this happening? I could hardly believe what I was hearing.

"Oh," Reina said, letting her arms fall to her side.

"As I was telling James, you two are the future of Rislandia. Your joy, your enthusiasm, your *love* is what matters in this kingdom. It's more important than airships, it's more important than the Atreblans, it's even more important than me."

I snuck a glance at Reina. Despite her tears, she was beaming with happiness. I must have been, too. I wanted to run and embrace her right there, but that might have put the king in an awkward position.

"If this is what you want," he said, probing Reina with his eyes.

"It is. I love James," she said. Her voice was so firm in the proclamation that I barely could keep myself from falling over. She hadn't told me this, but I'd known. I was glad to be right.

"Very well. James, take care of my daughter. Especially when I'm recovering. We'll talk again later." King Malaky's head drooped. He looked so weary.

"I will," I said, standing and taking my place by Princess Reina's side. "I always will. You can count on me, your Majesty."

PART III
HAZING

RISLANDIAN TIMELINE NOTES

The events in this story take place after The Fight For Rislandia.

CHAPTER 1

The sound of footfalls in the apprentice dormitory hallway jolted me awake. Ever since the Wyranth had invaded Rislandia City, I found myself sleeping lighter than before. I'd always been a light sleeper, but now when I woke, it was like someone doused me with cold water and shook me awake.

I instinctively reached for a sword by my bed but did not find it. It had been weeks since I'd been on guard duty, given weapons above my status of apprentice. Back at the Crystal Spire, training as a knight, they didn't allow us our own swords. I cursed under my breath. What a stupid rule. If Rislandia City was under attack again, I'd need a weapon.

It was dark in my quarters—a room with two bunk beds to sleep four apprentices. I slept on the bottom bunk across from the door. Reggie typically occupied the bunk across from me, but he wasn't there. I stood, looking to the top beds. The other two apprentices weren't there either. What was going on?

More footsteps sounded in the hallway, followed by a voice and a *shhh* sound.

I stepped out into the hall only to be grabbed by the collar of my shirt. The fabric constricted on my neck as I stumbled to the side—

directly into my attacker. I kicked back at him, forcing him to release his grip from me.

"Get him!" a gruff and muffled voice said.

The hallways were dark, none of the gas lamps on after curfew. There were at least four attackers near me, maybe more. They had on dark robes, making them blend in with the shadows, but they had white masks on. Were these Wyranth assassins?

I opened my mouth to yell, but one of the attackers wrapped a cloth tightly around my face. The cloth dampened the sound, gagging me. No one would hear me scream.

The attacker held the cloth around the back of my head while others grabbed for my arms. "We're going to need to grab his legs too. He's a kicker," the first one said.

They'd secured my arms faster than I could move, but I did manage to deliver a kick to one of their faces, forcing him to fall back into yet more dark robed figures. There were a lot more than I origi-nally anticipated, at least ten of them. I'd have no chance against this many, but I would go down fighting and take as many down with me as I could.

Which turned out to be zero, as two of the attackers managed to secure my legs, sweeping me off my feet and grabbing my legs in the air. I tried to kick and flail my way out of their grips, but these men were too strong.

"Stop resisting," the first said, pressing sword against my throat.

I didn't want to be captured. I'd rather die than give the Wyranth any information. But my struggling didn't seem to do me any good. Having woken up in the middle of the night, I didn't have the energy to resist further. I went slack in the men's arms.

"Take him away," the gruff voice said, pulling his sword back to allow his men passage.

They carried me out of the hallway.

* * *

THE STRANGE MASKED men took me out through the courtyard. I wish

I could shout or make some other noise to alert the other knights. Where had everyone gone, anyway? It was odd to see my roommates gone from our quarters, but they might have been called away on a mission. That explanation didn't sit right with me, though. Why wasn't I alerted if there was an important enough of a mission to take away all of the apprentice knights?

They carried me face up, leaving me to stare at the moon shining down on me in the freezing air of Rislandian winter. A chill bit through my bones, as I wore only my thin night clothes. I could see some of the rooftops of the buildings in Rislandia City, the ones that still stood after the brutal Wyranth assault. Much of the population of the city still hadn't returned, leaving the open areas even quieter than they usually would have been at this time of night, though I heard the whir of horseless carriages in the distance. It was going to be a hard winter of rebuilding, even if we could manage to get the supplies and foodstuffs we needed. With our country's only airship having crashed in the fateful battle, we hardly had the means to ask other countries for aid.

The attackers brought me through the courtyard, not seeming to be in any hurry. They didn't even appear worried about being spotted. I craned my neck to try to see how many enemies I faced. Their numbers were even worse than I'd thought in the hallway. Twenty or more. It would take a large force of knights to deal with this many invaders.

My assailants didn't take me to the city gates, but instead, they carried me toward the giant Crystal Spire which overlooked our city. The tallest building in Rislandia, and perhaps all of The Areth continent, it had been constructed hundreds of years ago as a lookout tower and a monument to Rislandian ingenuity.

They brought me inside the entrance to the tower and paused. This would be my chance. They'd get tired carrying me up the hundreds of stairs that spiraled all the way up to the top. I might be able to get them to drop me and make a run for it.

"Bind his hands and make him walk ahead of us," their gruff leader said. "I don't want to carry him up the stairs."

So much for the idea of escaping. My attackers set me down, and one of the masked men produced rope, tying my hands behind my back. Another one of them had a strange ruffled shirt—the kind used when people came to have an audience with the king. It looked ridiculous, and the one they brought me was a women's blouse. What was going on? I struggled, but they forced the blouse on me. I must have looked like an idiot.

The others pulled back, blocking the exit but leaving me to myself. I scanned the room, trying to find any way out, but there weren't any. One of the men had a camera on a wooden tripod. He tugged on a line, and a flashbulb went off brightly in my face. Why were they documenting this? I don't think I'd ever even had a picture taken of me before.

Too many of the masked men crowded into the tower behind me. I wouldn't be able to kick my way out. Resisting would be hopeless. Gas lamps lit the spiral staircases even through the night. The leader pointed the tip of his sword at me. "Up," he commanded.

Grumbling, I trudged up the stairs. It would be a long trek up to the top, and I worked about what they'd do to me. Were they going to throw me over the edge? Did they have a flying contraption to be able to whisk me out of here? The only other peoples with flying machines I'd seen were the Nightmen from Zenwey with their steam-powered bat-gliders. But they were far across the ocean. I doubted a small force of them would have broken into Rislandia City.

The masked men followed me up the stairs in dead silence, adding to the eerie atmosphere. A sense of dread filled me. I found myself sweating even though it was freezing cold. Between my nerves and the walk, it was too hot of a situation. We ascended the rest of the steps up to the platform that overlooked the city. When I reached the opening, a bright light shone in my face, not allowing me to see anything. One of the masked men flung a hood over my head, leaving me in utter darkness after they'd nearly blinded me.

My attackers led me forward and forced me to my knees.

* * *

"REMOVE THE BLINDFOLD," a commanding voice said.

The cloth came off of my head. I found myself before a small altar, a gas lamp burning on it with exhaust coming out the sides, creating a steamy atmosphere atop the Crystal Spire. On the platform rested a long, wooden box with a brass lock. From my kneeling position, I couldn't see above the stone railing which prevented people from plummeting to their deaths while up here.

The men in white masks and black cloaks surrounded me. I couldn't see their faces, but the masks gave them a ghastly look. Had I been targeted by a cult? I'd never seen anything of the like in all my years, but being from the country, perhaps I didn't spot some of the strange elements here. I was confident these weren't Wyranth, but what was going on? Were these people going to make me a blood sacrifice? I didn't want to die.

"James Gentry," the commanding voice said. "You've been accused of multiple accounts of protecting Rislandia from enemies foreign and domestic. This includes breaking into the Wyranth capital city and freeing prisoners from their dungeon, rooting out a spy within the knights and bringing him to justice, and finally felling a plot to assassinate King Malaky. How do you plea to these charges?" The man who spoke reached into his cloak and produced a sword. He brought it to my face and cut the gag out of my mouth.

These were odd charges. I didn't quite understand the way they phrased them. It made me rethink the identity of these masked men. Only Wyranth could be putting me on trial for defending Rislandia. But the way they phrased it made no sense. I just wanted to be back in my bunk, sleeping. This night was like a terrible nightmare. "I've done all of the above, but they're not crimes!" I said.

The group of masked men muttered amongst themselves. What were they deliberating?

The leader placed the flat of his sword on my shoulder. He took his off-hand and removed his mask.

I gasped when I saw who stood in front of me. It was Cid—the master knight who trained me from the first moment I'd arrived in

Rislandia City. Was he part of this strange cult? It made even less sense. A broad smile crossed his face.

Others removed their masks. Ethan, Tanner, and others I recognized from the mess hall. All journeymen other than Cid. I was more confused than ever. The knights had been turned against me!

Cid moved his sword to my opposite shoulder, tapping me with it. The wind picked up ominously, whistling and blowing the flag of Rislandia to the west. "By the authority invested in me by the High Knight and King Malaky, I grant you a promotion to journeyman knight."

The others clapped and hollered. Ethan moved to my back to undo the binds around my hands.

"Rise, Journeyman Gentry," Cid said. "You earned it."

I stood. The other journeymen slapped me on the back and congratulated me. This whole situation confused me so much.

Cid stepped to the side. "Open the case," he said, pointing to the box on the altar.

I pushed myself to my feet and stepped forward to the altar. The gas lamp flickered in the wind. I turned the key in the lock, and it clicked open.

Inside the case was a sword. It twinkled under the light of the gas lamp. I picked it up. It was lighter than the ones I'd used when out on missions, perfectly balanced. The hilt was engraved with the familiar symbols of a gear and wings—the crest of King Malaky.

"This is your sword, James, forged for you specifically as a knight. Take it, treasure it, and treat it as if it were your family, and the sword will guide you through the trials ahead," Cid said.

The others gave me a wide berth, allowing me to swing the sword —*my sword*—in the air. I could hardly believe it. I'd been worried for nothing! I couldn't help but laugh.

"The look in your eyes," Tanner said, chuckling along with me. "You were so scared. And we have a picture of it forever."

"That kick hurt," Ethan said.

"Sorry," I said, giving him a sheepish look. "Do you do this to everyone?"

"All the journeymen go through the ritual," Ethan said. "I'll show you my picture sometime. I looked like I'd seen a ghost!"

I couldn't take my eyes off my sword. Everything I'd ever hoped for had come true. These were my friends, despite their strange ritual. I belonged with the knights. "Thanks," I said.

Cid patted me on the shoulder. "You earned it, James. Now let's get you back to bed. We'll celebrate in the mess tomorrow with cake."

All the cloaked knights funneled back into the stairwell. I looked out over the kingdom of Rislandia, the kingdom I would protect with my life. We still had a lot of work to do, but I would stand by my brothers forever.

PART IV
SPY TRAINING

CHAPTER 1

"James, Ethan, come in. Thank you for arriving so quickly," Cid said, motioning Ethan and me into his office.

The older knight seemed to have aged in the last few months of the war. He didn't keep himself as neatly shaved as he used to—specks of white and gray hair sprinkled his shadowy beard. His eyes drooped, crow lines branching out from them.

We were all tired. Ever since I'd fled from Plainsroad Village during the first Wyranth attack, my life had been moving from one crisis to the next. The action had slowed a little since we retook Rislandia City and lost our kingdom's only airship in the process, but instead of taking a break, The Knights of the Crystal Spire took it upon ourselves to redouble our efforts in training.

Cid needed as many knights as possible for the coming battles, which very well could be even bloodier and more taxing than the beginnings of this war. After all, we didn't have an airship to soften the enemy up anymore.

"Of course," Ethan von Lantern said. He had a sword holstered on one hip and a pistol on another—the mark of a full Knight of the Crystal Spire. He'd been promoted soon after I was raised to the journeyman rank, allowing him to lord over me yet again. It had been a nice couple of weeks of being equals. I hoped I'd make full knight soon, if only so Ethan wouldn't be able to boss me around anymore.

Ethan had a slightly more muscular build than I did, and was taller, too. In a lot of ways, everything I could do, he could do better. He deserved the rank, even if my hunger for it made me a little jealous.

Another person sat in Cid's office with us, not a fellow knight, but a Lieutenant in the Grand Rislandian Army. He was short compared to the rest of us, and slightly overweight, but not fat. He had dark brown hair, which looked to be receding just a little on his forehead. Lieutenant Edwin Ral, the pilot of the former airship, *Liliana*. I hadn't seen him since our long journey to the strange Zenwey continent. As pilot, he didn't leave the bridge much, so I hadn't gotten to know him as well as some of the other crew.

"I don't suppose I need to introduce Lieutenant Ral to either of you?" Cid asked.

We shook our heads.

"Hey, Ethan, James," Ral said.

"Good," Cid said, leaning over his desk and folding his hands atop it. "I'm afraid I'm going to have to recall you from your training for a new mission. Hopefully, you're refreshed and ready to go."

Training often made me more tired than action, but I didn't need to press the point. The truth was, I'd be happy to get out of Rislandia City and back into interesting work.

Before this, I'd been set to guard Princess Reina, which ended up being more exciting than it should have with an assassination attempt on her father, but I hated standing guard, watching, waiting. Maybe it came from years of farm work, but I liked being on the move, occupied. Standing still didn't come naturally to me.

"We're ready as we'll ever be," Ethan said, speaking on our behalf.

"Good," Cid said. "Your next assignment's going to take you to Loveridge."

"That's still behind enemy lines, isn't it?" I asked. During the last major battle I'd parkten in, we'd taken back Irslandia City from the Wyranth, but they still held much of our land in their clutches.

Our forces had advanced into Greenhorne recently, but we hadn't been able to push past the Wyranth lines beyond the town. That was my understanding, unless I'd missed some news. Though in recent days, I'd kept pretty up to date on Rislandian matters, given I spent so much time with the princess.

"It is," Cid said. "You've posed as a Wyranth soldier before, when breaking into the prison with me to rescue Baron von Monocle."

"And again, when we discovered the Wyranth serum mine a few months ago," Ethan said.

Cid nodded. "You both have the experience needed to infiltrate. You won't be spending too much time with the Wyranth soldiers proper, if all goes well. You'll get in and out of Loveridge as quickly as possible."

Cid was being coy. I did't know why he didn't just tell us what the assignment was going to be. Could it be because of the danger involved? He didn't want to risk us but probably had no choice. In a lot of ways, Cid treated us like we were his children more than just soldiers. It had its benefits and its drawbacks.

"We're happy to serve however is needed," Ethan said.

Cid unfolded a map of the Loveridge region, setting it down on his desk. The town was a small one, which felt funny for me to think. Plainsroad Village, my hometown, barely warranted being mentioned on a map. Loveridge was much bigger, and as a young farm boy, I'd thought it was the pinnacle of civilization, but since my time traveling, I'd seen real cities. Loveridge had a single Main Street for the commercial part of town, with houses scattered in the forest beyond. Not much to it compared to Rislandia City.

"Here's the general area," Cid said. He pointed to a spot in the north. "The bulk of the Wyranth troops are stationed here." He dragged his finger around to the east. "If you circle around this way, you can avoid most of their army and enter without any problems. We've got Wyranth uniforms and travel papers ready for you, so you can act as if you're scouts patrolling the area."

"Once there," Cid continued, "you're going to be looking for the work of a Dr. Metzengerstein, a scientist from Nyanzi, who we believe has been providing the Wyranth with different technological and biological advantages in the recent campaign."

"Biological?" I asked.

Cid glanced to Ral. "I think you'd best handle this one."

The pilot sat up a little straighter in his chair as if he'd been off in his own world during the discussion so far. "Yes," he said. "I came across the doctor's work nearly three years ago when we'd first retired the *Liliana* to the Loveridge forest. He's not Rislandian, though he keeps a laboratory here. It seems he has been altering people to fuse them with different animalistic traits. It sounds crazy, but I know what I saw."

Ethan blinked. "What did you see?"

"A woman with extra, spider-like arms," Ral said, shivering. "The sight of spiders gives me the creeps to this day."

A woman mixed with a spider? It sounded absurd. However, I'd seen giant bats with hands and feet, and the strange blue Nightmen on the Zenwey continent, not to mention real giants. How could I question his story? Ral didn't seem like the type to make things up.

"We haven't been able to verify Ral's specific claims," Cid said, "but we've built an intelligence file on the doctor since then, which seems to corroborate his story. He's been involved with human experimentation. We believe he's the one responsible for creating the giant's blood serum the Wyranth soldiers have used to their advantage during their most recent advances. New reports indicate he's met with top-ranking Wyranth officials in Loveridge in recent days."

Ral tapped his fingers on the desk. "We've also heard rumors that the Iron Emperor has obtained airship design plans, which disappeared from the *Liliana* when it crashed. It's unclear if the two events are related, but our engineers are having trouble rebuilding the ship without plans. You'll need to retrieve any information on Wyranth experiments on humans or with airships you can find."

Cid nodded. "Can you tell us a little more of what you know of the location?"

"His lab was just south of the main town, off a dirt path to the right, disguised as a small farm and house. You can't miss it because the forest thins out. Last I saw," Ral said, "the barn was in flames. The whole thing was burning down when I'd left. I reported everything to General Cartwright at the time, but I don't think he ever sent someone to investigate this strange scientist."

Cid glanced between us. "It'll be on you to investigate. If the Wyranth are developing something new, we need to know about it."

I clapped my hands together. "You can count on us, sir."

Ethan grinned. "Sounds like it'll be a good time. When do we leave?"

"We'll get you fitted with Wyranth uniforms and prepare you for departure tomorrow morning," Cid said.

"Good luck," Ral said, biting on his lower lip. "I hope you don't run into any spidery women."

I hoped we wouldn't either. The Wyranth would be enough of a challenge for us to deal with. But I didn't mind. It would be good to get back to real knight work again.

CHAPTER 2

I STOOD IN FRONT OF THREE LARGE MIRRORS, TWO ANGLED TOWARD ME, and one facing me straight on. The tailor worked at the seams on my ankles, marking with different pins while I could do nothing but stare at myself.

My hair was getting a little long, light brown bangs falling into my eyes. I'd bulked up in muscle during the last few months. Honestly, I looked impressive. I smirked to the mirror.

"I know that look, James Gentry," a feminine voice said from behind me.

Her reflection appeared in the mirror. Elegant blonde tresses fell just over the bodice of a baby blue dress that accented her eyes. It fit her form so perfectly. The tailor had clearly designed it for her. I was glad he did. It was all I could do not to let my jaw go slack.

The sight of Princess Reina stilled my heart every time she appeared. It didn't matter that I saw her every day since being assigned to guard her. I'd never get used to her intense beauty. It was hard to believe she was real. Even crazier, she *liked* me.

"Uh, what look?" I asked. I did my best not to let my voice crack, but my throat was so dry.

"The one where you're contemplating trouble," she said.

"Oh," I said.

She nodded to herself as if proud she'd rooted something out of me. She came closer to the podium while the tailor worked, tugging at the end of the fabric of the Wyranth soldier's jacket. "Their uniforms are almost as oppressive as they are. I'm glad our flag at least gives a little flair with the gear and wings symbol."

The crest of her house. I liked the look of it as well, but having grown up seeing the flag everywhere, I supposed I was biased.

"All right," the tailor said, interrupting the thought. He stepped back to take a look. "I believe that will look about right on you. Where's the next boy?"

"Present," Ethan said, entering the dressing room a moment after speaking. "It's a bit crowded in here, isn't it?"

"We won't be in here much longer," Reina said, hooking her arm under mine. "James and I will go for a walk while we wait for Ethan to get measured. Isn't that right, James?"

My face became hot, but I wasn't sure why. "Uh…yeah. We'll do that," I said.

As Reina dragged me backward, Ethan stepped on the platform to get his Wyranth uniform fitted. I caught him making a kissy face at me through the mirror. My face must have reddened even more.

Like he was one to judge me. He was just as head over heels for Zaira von Monocle, airship captain extraordinaire and my best friend before all of this knight craziness began. Everyone always said she and I would get married one day, but all that changed when I got entangled with the princess.

We walked through the corridors of the royal palace. We'd been able to use the royal tailor for the job to make sure we had the best work done for our mission. Various servants and attendants went wide-eyed as they saw the princess with someone in a Wyranth uniform.

"You could have let me change first, at least," I said.

Reina brought me over to a sitting room with plush couches made of red fabric. The corner of the room had a vase with tall exotic flowers in it, and a brilliant, colorful tapestry with a rendition of the

Crystal Spire hung on the wall. Reina released me and closed the door behind her.

I stood there like a buffoon, both confused and in awe of her beauty. Her eyes held such fire in them, such passion. For me? What did I ever do to deserve such a blessing?

Instead of an answer, I was greeted by Reina rushing to press herself against me. I wrapped my arms around her, dutifully holding her close. Her hair smelled of jasmine, a beautiful scent I could breathe in for eternity if she would let me. But she didn't arrange this meeting so I could ogle her. I knew what she wanted.

I leaned my head in. She closed her eyes and parted her lips eagerly. We kissed. A good, long kiss. Our tongues met. Even the way she kissed was dainty and beautiful. Her mouth was warm, and I fast became warm all over. I squeezed her closer to me.

Moments later, we came up for air.

She shivered. "James, you're amazing."

"No, you're amazing," I countered.

We stared at each other, and then we both broke into laughter.

"People must think we're so stupid," Reina said.

"I don't really care what they think. I want to go to the top of the Crystal Spire and shout your name," I said.

Reina smiled. "Save me some of your passion for when you get back."

Get back. The mission, right. It had been a long time since I'd been assigned to a mission that would take me away from her. The last time was when I'd traveled to the Zenwey continent on the *Liliana*.

Reina and I had barely known each other then. We'd exchanged a few kisses, but it wasn't like now. Now, it felt like I had to rip my heart out and leave it here. A sense of dread filled my chest.

Reina noticed. I could tell by the way her eyes softened. "I've worried you, haven't I? Oh, I'm sorry. You'll do fine, James. I know you will. I have faith in you."

"This'll be a dangerous one," I said softly.

Reina nodded, and then pressed her head against my shoulder.

I ran my hand through her hair, enjoying the sensation of her breathing on my neck. It tickled, but in a good way. "At least it's not halfway across the world like last time. I shouldn't be gone too long."

"I hope not," Reina said, "but I wanted to see you before you left, regardless."

I wasn't sure what I should say afterward, so I stood and held her. We naturally rocked back and forth after a time, like slow dancing but to no music. Time slowed, and I didn't want it to end.

Reina lifted her head. I took the opportunity to lay another kiss on her. She was eager. My hands drifted to her waist.

A noise sounded. The door handle jingled, and the hinge creaked. Someone opened the door.

Reina jumped backward, placing a hand on her chest. She turned to see one of the palace servants. "Joel, you scared the daylights out of me," she said.

The servant blushed, casting his eyes aside. It was clear he didn't want to cause the princess any embarrassment. "I'm sorry, Princess," he said. "King Malaky sent me to retrieve you. His fever is worsening, and he wants to see you. I didn't know you were, uh, indisposed."

I scratched my head, embarrassed at the awkward situation, but I was also worried about King Malaky. A fever? "I should probably be getting back to the tailor, anyway. He probably needs the uniform back to do his alterations."

Reina nodded. "Could you give us a second, Joel?"

The servant bowed his head, stepped outside, and closed the door.

"What's wrong with your father?" I asked, my thoughts drifting back to the king.

"Oh, it's nothing to worry about. He's been feeling ill the past few days. He just needs some rest," she said. Her voice wavered, however. She was nervous but was trying to put on a good front. Whether it was because she didn't want to worry me before my mission, or she was trying to hope for the best, I couldn't tell. But there was something wrong.

I couldn't call her on it. Not now. I merely nodded. "Okay," I said. "I'm glad I got to see you at least."

"Me, as well," Reina said.

I took her hands into mine and squeezed. "I love you," I said.

"I love you, too."

Her fingertips dragged off mine, touching me in an elegant and sensual way. I could have melted then.

She turned to the door, giving me one final glance over her shoulder before looking back. "You stay safe," she said. Then, she opened the door and departed with the servant.

I made my way back into the tailor's chamber, where Ethan had already changed back into his typical attire of browns and leathers. He grinned wickedly at me as I returned. "How was it?" he asked patronizingly.

I narrowed my eyes, stepped up to him, and shoved him.

Ethan laughed and held his hands up. The tailor looked at me as if I were crazy but didn't say anything.

"I'm just teasing," Ethan said.

"I know," I said. I sounded like I was pouting. I didn't know what made me so defensive about it.

"You'd best get her off your mind before tomorrow, though. You're gonna need to focus on this mission. We have to pretend to be Wyranth soldiers, after all."

"I'll be fine, *Hans*," I said. It was the name on the forged travel papers Ethan had.

"I'm sure you will, *Klaus*," Ethan said.

We'd decided to try to use the names as much as possible to get used to them. But they were so odd, so foreign. How did the Wyranth use those names? I couldn't quite fathom it. Even though he was teasing me, Ethan was right. I was going to have to focus on making sure we succeeded in this mission.

I couldn't afford to worry about Reina, or King Malaky for that matter. Part of me wanted to tell Ethan I'd found out the king was ill, but I thought better of it. He didn't need to bear the burden of such knowledge before heading out on a mission. It would have been better if I'd not seen Reina at all.

CHAPTER 3

WE HITCHED A RIDE ON A HORSELESS CARRIAGE ON OUR WAY OUT OF THE capital city before dawn. Our army had recently advanced on Greenhorne, which was just down the road from Plainsroad Village, my hometown. They'd cut off the Wyranth near my village in the process, and we were able to ride there safely.

It's where the carriage stopped, as we would be traveling through the forest by foot with Loveridge due south, the road veering toward the west. We hoped to avoid the main line so the Wyranth wouldn't spot us—and also so our own people wouldn't see us and mistakenly shoot at us.

The sun crept over the horizon when we reached Plainsroad Village. Our driver slowed and finally stopped just where the old schoolhouse had been.

I hopped out of the carriage, slinging my pack over my shoulder, and made for the spot.

My heart sank into my stomach. My hands became sweaty and balmy. I clutched at the fabric of my Wyranth uniform, needing something to hold onto from what I saw.

It had been razed to the ground. Only embers and wreckage remained where I'd spent hours upon hours in a classroom. I recalled

Mrs. Everley writing out math lessons on the chalkboard. I used to wad up bits of paper and spit them at the back of Zaira's head.

Once, she'd gotten so mad she'd turned around and tackled me right out of my chair. The whole class laughed and mocked us when we were on the ground, her atop me.

I decided it would be best not to tell Ethan that story.

My memories were so vivid, burned into my mind as deeply as the char from the remains of the schoolhouse.

By the schoolhouse was the market square where my father used to sell our farm goods to traveling merchants up and down the road. Tomatoes were our main crop, but we also grew potatoes and grains, and we sold chickens and cows from time to time. I'd help him on days when I didn't have school. I missed those days. I missed Da.

My knees became weak. They buckled.

I landed on hard-packed dirt, pain flaring in my kneecaps, paling in comparison to the immense torture in my chest.

It hadn't been all that long ago since I departed Plainsroad Village. A fateful night where the Wyranth war engines *clacked* their way forward until their barrage of armaments attacked my home.

I hadn't seen the worst of it. My father had told me to take Zaira and go on the family horse, Lightning, and get as far away as possible. The fear in his eyes had been so intense, I had no choice but to obey.

The Wyranth destroyed our home. They killed my parents. Over the months, I did everything I could to hold the feelings back, to forget Ma and Da. I put my all into becoming a knight—the best knight possible—in order to push aside what had happened. I worked hard to forget.

Part of me wanted to never return to Plainsroad Village. Everything here served as a reminder of the life I'd had, of the loving parents who did their best to raise me. The home cooked meals, the camaraderie of working together in the fields, the washed clothes— they were all gone now. I'd taken them for granted then. It was all the Wyranths' fault.

I dug my fingers into the dirt, picking up several pebbles and a handful of the rocky substance.

"Are you okay?" Ethan asked.

I cocked my arm back and flung the dirt toward the broken structure that was formerly the schoolhouse. While doing so, I let out the angriest yell, a gesture of pure rage. It wasn't fair. None of this was fair. The Wyranth took so much from all of us. How could this be allowed to happen?

The dirt scattered in the wind, some of the pebbles going so far as to hit the side of the razed schoolhouse. It was over now. The anger evaporated.

My body still felt shaky, hungry for something I couldn't quite grasp. It didn't matter, but it did make this mission all the more important.

We could never let the Wyranth succeed in their torment of Rislandians again.

The view of my old town served as a reminder we weren't just following some orders, but this war was personal.

"James?" Ethan asked again, sounding concerned.

I pushed myself to my feet. Ethan grabbed me by the arm and helped me most of the way until I could steady myself. Once upright, I bent over to dust myself off. "Sorry," I said.

"Don't be. I can only imagine how hard it must be—"

"It's nothing," I said.

Ethan watched me for a long moment, skepticism dripping from his face. He looked like he wanted to say something, but he shook his head.

"I won't press you," he said, "but I should remind you we're on an espionage mission. We don't want to draw attention to ourselves. If you feel the urge to yell like that again, you have to hold yourself back, understand?"

"Yeah," I said. It had been foolish, but it felt better getting it out. I wouldn't need to do it again.

"Good," Ethan said, motioning for me to follow him. He started down the road on foot, heading straight south to where the road would bend. We'd have to trudge through the tall grasses of the plains ahead.

The mission came first. Even if my memories haunted me, the best thing I could do now was to honor their memories by succeeding. I understood it intellectually, even if a large part of me wanted to stay in Plainsroad Village forever, lie down, and curl up in hopes my ma would somehow magically show up. She wouldn't. My thoughts weren't rational.

I exhaled a deep breath.

Ethan patted me on the shoulder. "I know I give you a hard time sometimes, but you're a good man."

His words caused me to raise my chin in a little bit of pride. "You think so?" I didn't know why I felt so vulnerable, why I craved Ethan's approval, but I did. It was embarrassing.

"I do." He glanced to the side of the road. "When you were up at Lake Avily, Zaira and I came here. Did she tell you about it?"

I shook my head. We continued walking.

"She seemed more shocked than upset. I guess it's a little different with her."

"Yeah," I said. She still had her father.

"She's been acting a lot more depressed lately," Ethan said. He stepped into the grasses, pushing some of the taller ones aside as he pressed onward.

I followed behind him. Zaira and I hadn't exactly been close since we'd admitted to each other that we had other romantic interests. I had Princess Reina, and Zaira had Ethan. It was best to leave it there.

It wasn't awkward seeing her or anything, but I didn't feel the inclination to spend time with her like I had when I was a kid. The sensation was so confusing, and I felt guilty for it. Girls made everything so complicated. "What do you mean?" I asked, not sure what else to say.

"You know how she usually has this energy about her? How it seems almost like she's buzzing around everyone else and we're just there slowing her down?"

I knew it well. I used to chuck tomatoes at her to try to bring her back to reality from her daydreaming. It worked most of the time, even if she got mad and started slapping me afterward. The thought made me smile. "Yeah."

"It's been gone lately. Like, ever since the airship crash, a little light's gone out inside of her. I can't place it." He clicked his tongue. "When we get back, I want to do something special for her. Been trying to figure something out for the last couple of weeks, but I realized she plays herself very close to the vest. I have no idea what she likes, what she doesn't. She's a lot like you in some ways, how you bury yourself in your training."

I shifted my pack. "You noticed that?"

"I notice a lot of things. It's why I keep getting promoted."

"Fair," I said, continuing slightly behind him to utilize the path he'd created between the tall grasses. "So, you want some information."

"Yeah."

"What're you going to give me in return?"

Ethan glanced back over his shoulder, giving me an irritated look. "Are you serious?"

"Hey, this is above and beyond my duties as a journeyman knight," I said.

"What do you want?" he asked.

"Hmm," I considered. What was the worst part of my existence at the moment? I snapped my fingers as it came to me. "When we get back, you could offer to cover my barracks floor cleaning duties." Journeymen had to take care of the cleaning for the full knights. I hated doing it.

"No way," Ethan said.

"Oh, well. Guess you don't love Zair-bear that much."

"Come on."

I held firm, silent. We were still a good ways from the cover of the forest up ahead, but no Wyranth appeared to be patrolling this area. With our main army line so close, they wouldn't likely be anywhere until we reached cover. We'd be in more danger of our own forces mistaking us for some rogue Wyranth infantrymen the way we were dressed.

Ethan sighed. "Fine. I'll do it."

I chuckled. "Zair-bear's always been about fancy things. She never got much growing up. Her da was always away, and though he sent back strange items from his travels, we were still off in the country. We didn't have a lot of the finer things. She's always had an eye for fancy dresses."

"Clothes?" Ethan stopped in his tracks, turned back to me again, and scrunched his nose. "That's it?"

"Trust me."

"Alright. It'd better be worth it," he said.

"I wouldn't steer you wrong."

We continued ahead, talking about girls, guns, and what we thought we'd do after the war ended. I realized I liked Ethan quite a bit. He was a good fit for Zaira. I was glad they found each other, and that I had him as a friend and mentor.

CHAPTER 4

SEVERAL HOURS LATER, WE'D MADE IT THROUGH THE THICK OF THE
forest. I kept asking Ethan if he was sure we were going the right way.
As the trees covered more of the sky and landscape, it became difficult
to get one's bearings, but he seemed confident. We had supplies
enough to keep us alive if we got lost, but I still didn't want to be faced
with the prospect.

Ethan proved to be able to navigate, and soon, we came upon some
structures, which we saw through the thick woods. We walked at a
normal pace, not trying to conceal ourselves. Dressed as a Wyranth
patrol, we acted like one. I touched the top of my metal helmet to
make sure it was secure. Loveridge came into full view.

It was a small town, one main street comprised of mostly log
buildings. Some were longer or wider, and a couple had paint, but the
construction matched the forest and resources around them. Even
though it was spring, and we were warm from walking for hours and
hauling large packs, the general forest was cool. Smoke and steam
came from various chimneys throughout the town.

The streets were muddy, and the buildings had a worn look to
them. Recent rains and the Wyranth invasion had taken its toll. As we
drew closer, it became apparent one of the doors of a nearby building

was tilted off a hinge, looking like it was rusted. The people of Loveridge had not maintained their town very well.

What struck me was the lack of people in the streets. It was daytime, which meant folk should be out working. Even in a small town like Plainsroad Village, farmers bustled around, moving feed, selling their goods, meeting with merchants.

Loveridge was bigger than my hometown. There were people here, given the smoke rising from the buildings, but where were they?

My answer came in the form of two Wyranth soldiers walking down the street. They grew in my field of vision as they came closer.

"Act as if you're walking by my side, back from a patrol," Ethan said in a low tone. He changed his posture and his walk to stand a little straighter. His acting skills weren't so bad.

I hoped I could match him. I tried to keep pace, each step with his like we were trained to march together. While it wasn't a difficult task, I was overthinking it, and it made me nervous. My fingers dug into my palms. They were slick with sweat.

"Don't worry so much. Act like you know what you're doing," Ethan said.

"I'm trying," I whispered.

The Wyranth came closer. Opposite us stood two men in dark uniforms. Once had a pointy chin, with stubble growing in patches on his face. The other looked too fat to be a soldier. I couldn't imagine someone fighting with his girth. His uniform seemed to want to burst at the buttons. The two men stopped in front of us.

"Are you new here?" the pointy-chinned Wyranth asked.

"Yes, just shifted patrols," Ethan said. He held out his papers. "Here's our orders."

The man read the papers, and then looked up at us. "Sergeant, Major, we're glad to have you," he said.

I relaxed my shoulders, my pack's weight suddenly feeling very heavy. At least they weren't suspicious of us.

"I'm Corporal Gustaaf, and this is Sergeant Bram," the pointy-chinned man said, motioning to the man next to him.

Bram gave a little grunt. The Wyranth must have been desperate for men to press into service. There was no way he could run fast, and he didn't seem very personable. What did he have to offer the military?

I shouldn't complain. If the Wyranth didn't have their best coming after us, this war would go a lot more smoothly.

"Where'd you transfer from?" Gustaaf asked.

"The line," Ethan said.

The men across from us frowned, looked at each other, and then back to us. "I'm sorry to hear that. It must be hard."

"We fight as the Iron Emperor commands," Ethan said. His words sounded much more calculated than usual.

"Does he speak?" Bram, the fat man, asked, inclining his chin toward me.

Ethan looked at me expectantly.

"Of course I do," I said. The words came out a little too rushed. My tongue was dry. This whole espionage thing made me far too nervous. I was a straight-talking farm boy. I could fight with the best of them, but this felt far too much like lying. It didn't sit well.

Gustaaf didn't seem to notice. His gaze shifted toward the forest, distant in his thoughts. "We are just about to head out on patrol. It would be good if you'd join us. We may not have the troubles the line does, but we have our own issues. We could use some help."

"Happy to oblige," Ethan said.

I wanted to protest. We had a job to do. We didn't need to get caught up in whatever the Wyranth were doing. We had to find this Dr. Metzengerstein, or information about him, and get out of there. A quick mission and run back home. The longer we lingered, the more the Wyranth might start asking questions we wouldn't be able to answer.

But I deferred to Ethan. He had earned my trust. I hoped he was making the right call here.

The two Wyranth slipped around us and continued down the main road of Loveridge. Stones lined the streets, protruding from the mud. They must have had some rain here in recent days.

We turned and followed them. Gustaaf and Bram split, flanking us.

It made me uncomfortable being in between the two of them, putting them at an advantage if they decided we needed to be captured. Still, I tried to face forward, focusing my eyes on trees ahead so I wouldn't side-glance with suspicion.

"What's troubling you here?" Ethan asked. "Locals causing a scene?"

"Nothing like that. The Rislandians are docile people," Gustaaf said as we walked. "I doubt they would be able to mount an insurrection even if their fabled knights showed in the city."

I kept my mouth clamped tightly shut.

"No," Gustaaf said, "it's our own who are the problems. You're aware of the serum the first through fifth legions were given in order to boost their capacities as soldiers?"

"I heard of it," Ethan said.

"We are without a supply of it because the Rislandians have destroyed our sources. And without it, some soldiers go berserk. We're dealing with those rogue soldiers now. There's some out there, and they're just as liable to attack us as anyone else. It's our job to find and incapacitate them so they don't cause us any further trouble."

"Trouble?" I asked. "Did something happen?"

Bram let out a sigh. "One attacked the commandant two nights ago in the town's tavern. He came running in and bit the commandant in the shoulder, taking out a good chunk of his flesh. I was enjoying libations at the time. It was a disturbing sight."

"Awful," Ethan said.

"Worse, the commandant contracted rabies. He began foaming at the mouth. A fever overcame him yesterday. He's unconscious now, and we're not sure he's going to make it," Gustaaf said.

"I hope he does," I said.

"Me, as well." Bram chuckled. "Though, it is nice not having his oversight. We've gotten to spend a little more time off our feet than usual."

Gustaaf elbowed him in the side. "You shouldn't tell new soldiers that. It will erode discipline."

"I assure you, you don't have to worry about discipline with us," Ethan said.

Gustaaf led the team deeper into the forest. Unlike when we'd entered Loveridge, we moved cautiously, trying not to make too much sound with each step.

The sounds of the forest became clearer. Birds chirped and flapped their wings. Animals made strange noises. The wind blew gently through the leaves of the trees.

A twig snapped.

In an uncanny motion, Bram lowered his rifle and fired.

I found myself surprised at how much I admired the Wyranth's abilities with a gun. It was as if his rifle extended from his arm, and his motion came from him with a fluidity one would expect from a gazelle. He had closed one eye in the process, and when the shot rang out, he opened the corner of his mouth and spit something on the ground.

The sound of the forest died.

"You get it?" Gustaaf asked.

"Think so," Bram said.

He slung his rifle over his shoulder, and we walked forward. A fallen tree trunk lay across our path, rotted in some parts. Moss covered a part of it. A small blast mark was scorched into the top of it.

Bram bent over the trunk, reaching behind it. When his hand lifted, he held a dead squirrel by the tail. He laughed heartily. "It will learn not to make any more noise, eh?"

"You never cease to amaze me. Now put that thing down," Gustaaf said.

Bram shrugged his pack off his shoulder and opened the top of it with his free hand.

"You have to be kidding me," Gustaaf said.

"Never waste a good meal," Bram said.

Ethan and I looked at each other. His lips pinched tightly together as if he tried not to laugh. I was trying not to laugh, as well.

"You know," Ethan said, a twinkle forming in his eye, "I heard there was some mad scientist about these woods. I was worried the sound might have been one of his experiments run amok. Do you know anything about it?"

Gustaaf plugged his nose as if to evade the stench of the dead squirrel. Bram looked content.

"I heard of a strange man at a farm to the south of the town," Gustaaf said. "Some of the officers go there sometimes. I haven't heard of any strange contraptions coming out of there, though."

Ethan shrugged. "Well, I guess we're safe for now."

The south of the town. That gave us a place to look whenever we could get away from these two.

My thoughts were interrupted by another rustling sound, crackling deep in the forest beyond. The sun was beginning to set in the late afternoon, shadows obscuring much of the near forest from sight.

Gunshots sounded, and they didn't come from Bram.

CHAPTER 5

Bullets flew. I took cover behind one of the trees. Ethan went for another. The two Wyranth with us dropped behind the fallen trunk.

"Rislandians or our people?" Bram asked.

"Ours," Ethan said. "I can see the shine of their helmets." He grabbed his rifle and fired in the direction the shots had come from. Whether he could get a good look or he was trying to keep them at bay, I couldn't tell.

I gripped my rifle. It was much heavier than the pistols I'd practiced with, but I'd become proficient enough of a shooter over the course of this war. I still fought better with a sword, but unless we were in close quarters, it wouldn't be possible.

Our Wyranth companions aimed and fired. Someone shouted in pain in the distance.

"I'd say you got one," Gustaaf said.

"When do I ever miss?" Bram asked.

Gustaaf snorted and reloaded his gun.

I spotted the other Wyranth between the trees. The glimmer of their helmets gave them away. Who had designed those? They made soldiers into easy targets. Easier than they would have been ordinarily.

Our targets were still far off. I did my best to get them between my sights, but with them on the move and too many trees in the way, I fired a shot that blasted bark off a tree trunk. "Gah," I said to myself. Even though this wasn't a competition, I wanted to prove myself valuable with the firearm.

The two enemies in the forest fired back at us. Ethan and I pressed ourselves to the trees, careful not to give them any targets. We wore the same uniforms as our enemies, our helmets shining just as much as theirs. I had to remember that and keep my head behind the tree as much as possible.

Ethan gave me a signal, motioning his hand clockwise. He wanted me to sneak around and circle our targets. It made sense to me.

I darted to my left, giving myself a wide berth to do my best to get out of our targets' field of vision. They had to be occupied with the firing of our two Wyranth companions. A glance to the right, and I saw Ethan had vacated the spot he'd been hiding. He became a blur running into the forest.

For his plan to be most effective, we had to get there roughly at the same time. They would have nowhere to hide with bullets flying in every direction. It'd cause a panic. At least I hoped it would.

I tried to keep to the shadows, moving quickly, but also avoiding making noise. Bullets blasted back and forth, the cracking of gunshots echoing in the forest.

I came up alongside where the Wyranth made their stand. They used trees for cover just as Ethan and I did. Ethan's helmet poked from behind one of the trees. He was there, ready. We'd done it.

I leveled my rifle. The enemy was so much closer now, and they didn't see me. I fired. Ethan shot simultaneously. The gunfire from our allies continued.

The Wyranth closest to me jolted his hands upward, dropping his gun. My bullet had hit the stock, ricocheting into the tree beside him. He stumbled backward.

Ethan's target collapsed.

"Hold your fire!" Ethan shouted, running forward with his rifle in hand.

The lone Wyranth's eyes went wide. He backpedaled away from Ethan, but the effect of his movement drove him right into my path. He didn't even see me standing there waiting for him.

I turned my rifle to use the stock as a bludgeon. Using the power of both my arms, I cocked my arms to the side, taking a single lunge toward the Wyranth as I used my body's momentum to turn and swing.

Crack.

I smacked the Wyranth in the back. He fell to the forest floor, coughing. The blow had to be painful.

Ethan approached, putting his boot to the Wyranth's back to make sure he stayed down. "We got them," Ethan said.

Gustaaf and Bram came running up to us, slinging their rifles behind them as they came close. "You two are good," Gustaaf said.

"Why thank you," Ethan said. "Do you want him for interrogation?'

Bram laughed. "Have you never encountered one of these feral serum addicts before?"

Ethan and I looked at each other. We had. They had crazy eyes and attacked ferociously. We'd never had to deal with them from this perspective, though. What were we supposed to say?

"No, I haven't," Ethan said in a low tone.

"There's no reasoning with them. No way to heal them. They're lost," Gustaaf said. He motioned to me. "You've got your gun out. Put him down."

I blinked. "What?"

"Shoot him," Gustaaf said.

I'd killed before. It was part of my duty, but this was different. Beneath Ethan's boot lay a helpless man, squirming. I couldn't just execute someone like this. It made me think back to Plainsroad Village, and my ma and da having nothing they could do against the Wyranth. The lack of mercy they showed to them. Could I do the same in reverse? "Wouldn't it be better to at least try to get him to a medic?"

"Do you have a problem with hearing?" Gustaaf asked. He seemed to be getting annoyed with me.

"I..." I didn't know what to do. I froze, not wanting to kill this man. There had to be something we could do for him.

Before I could think of anything to say, Ethan had his gun trained right at the man's head. He pulled the trigger and blasted him right in the back of the neck, where the metal helmet receded.

I couldn't help but wince. The body writhed, and then stopped moving entirely.

The Wyranth frowned at me.

"I'm sorry," Ethan said. "Hans has seen too many of our compatriots lose their lives. It's taken a toll on him."

Bram frowned. "I can understand. Come, we can get food and drink back at the tavern in town and dull our senses."

"Sounds good," Ethan said. He slung his rifle over his shoulder and grabbed me by the arm. "Excuse me while I talk to my subordinate."

He pulled me off to the side. We veered away from the Wyranth soldiers, a couple of trees in between us as we made our way back toward town.

"What?" I asked.

"You need to get your act together," Ethan said, keeping his voice low. "The Wyranth are ruthless. If you start getting jittery, they're more likely to catch us."

"It wasn't necessary to kill that man."

"Not if he were among us, but with them, it's more important we act the part. If we get caught, it's going to be *us* they're shooting."

I thought about it. The whole thing didn't sit well with me, executing a helpless man. I didn't care whether it was needed to blend in or not.

Maybe I wasn't cut out for spying.

CHAPTER 6

"BOTTOMS UP!" BRAM SHOUTED, HOLDING A MUG OF BEER UP HIGH. Foam spilled over the top of it, dripping onto the wooden countertop of Loveridge's sole tavern. He didn't seem to mind. Nor did the other Wyranth drinking along with him.

The inside of the tavern looked much like the construction did on the outside—big, round logs stacked on one another, an A-frame ceiling, with more used as beams across the top. At the front door, there was a stuffed head of a bear, growling at all of us inside. Several tables littered the place, but most of the patronage sat at a long, wooden bar.

Ethan and I had our own cups of beer, though neither of us drank hard like the Wyranth soldiers after they *clanged* their glasses together. We needed to keep our wits about us. Besides, beer tasted disgusting. I'd tried it once when my da had a cup at the local market. He'd given me a sip. I spit it out immediately.

This stuff in the tavern smelled even worse than whatever I'd tasted back then. There was no way I'd drink it.

Gustaaf and Bram seemed friendly with most of the soldiers here. They knew everyone and introduced us to a few others. Ethan did most of the talking as he'd done the entire time we'd been here.

I wanted to ask more questions about this mad scientist's work.

No one in the tavern seemed worried about human experimentation. But would the Wyranth care anyway? They took the strange giant's serum at the command of their emperor, and none seemed to question the substance that drove their companions to berserk rage.

There were a few civilian residents of Loveridge in the tavern, beyond the couple working the bar. I snuck glances toward them. They seemed tired, haggard. I wanted to talk to them, but would Ethan chastise me for fraternizing with fellow Rislandians?

The soldiers seemed to keep to themselves, away from them.

"I wish we'd be stationed somewhere with more population," one of the soldiers said. He was a thin man with dark eyes. "Say what you will about Rislandians, but their women... Have you seen the von Monocle girl?"

"Are you serious, Vance?" Gustaaf asked, rolling his eyes. "You haven't had nearly enough to drink to be rambling about her *again*."

"You'd have to see her in person to understand. I was stationed in the palace when she was held captive. She had..." he motioned in front of his chest with both hands, cupping them in the air, forehead wrinkling as if in deep thought as he paused, "great assets."

The other Wyranth soldiers laughed.

Disgusting. I wanted to sock him in the face.

Ethan shot me a warning glance.

My fist tightened, but I willed myself to loosen my fingers. I wouldn't overreact here. They were just talking. There was nothing they could do.

"It's not like you would have wooed her with your ugly mug," Bram said.

"You're one to talk, chubby," Vance said.

"It's just more of me to love." Bram grabbed his stomach and jiggled it.

The other Wyranth burst into laughter again.

"I'm serious, though," Vance said. "You have to see her. More than just her supple body, there's something about her. It's captivating. If the Iron Emperor hadn't personally ordered the guards not to touch her..." He shook his head.

"Let's talk about something else," Gustaaf said. The conversation had taken a bit of a dark turn, and I could tell Gustaaf, at least, was a man of honor. "I've heard enough about von Monocles to last a lifetime."

"I've heard rumors they're demons," Bram said, downing the rest of his beer mug.

"I said I don't want to talk about them anymore," Gustaaf said, his voice firmer.

"I'm more curious about the scientist we were talking about earlier," Ethan said. He wasn't subtle at all. But did it matter with a bunch of drunken soldiers?

"The old kook? He isn't here very often," Vance said. He was the talker. Loose lips, at least when he was drunk. His eyes looked glazed over, and he struggled to stay atop his barstool. "Absolutely mad… though he's got a pretty assistant. Red hair that flows down to…" he made the cupping gesture by his chest again, "you know."

It was obvious what was on his mind.

"Lucky man, traveling with someone like that. I don't know what she sees in the spectacle-wearing fop," he said.

"Someone who has more smarts than you," one of the other soldiers said. Several of them laughed again.

"Who said that?" Vance stumbled to his feet, his eyes darting back and forth.

"Settle down," Bram said.

"You settle down!" Vance said. He turned to me.

I froze.

"You! Get that smug look off your face. You think you're so much better than me?" Vance wobbled over. He could barely stand up. Judging from the fire in his eyes, it was clear there would be no way he'd back down either.

I put my hands up all the same. "I don't know what you're talking about," I said.

"Leave the kid alone," Gustaaf said.

Vance didn't listen. He pressed forward and pushed me against the bar. I fell off my stool but gripped onto the bar so I wouldn't fall over completely.

The drunk Wyranth threw a punch. My eyes went wide as his fist sped toward my face. I ducked to the side.

His momentum carried him across the bar, his arm sliding down it and knocking over several drinks. Glass shattered. The bartenders stepped backward, too afraid to do anything about the Wyranth.

The other soldiers were of no help. Instead of trying to hold him back, they cheered him on.

I backed away from the bar, but a circle of Wyranth formed around us. I was trapped.

Vance spun around to face me. He barely could maintain his balance, but he was dead set on getting to me.

I raised my fists. What else could I do? I tried to glance out the corner of my eye at Ethan, but I couldn't spot him through the gathered crowd.

Another punch came my way.

I dodged again, sidestepping this time. Vance stumbled into several of the other soldiers.

It wasn't a fair fight. I was clear-headed, and he wasn't. When he turned around again, I socked him hard in the gut. His reaction time was slow, but his fists flew toward my head. I ducked, then swept his legs out from under him.

Vance hit the floor hard. He didn't get up.

Several of the Wyranth cheered. Others went to help their fallen friend. I received pats on the back.

"Good job, kid," Gustaaf said.

Ethan grabbed me by the arm, pulling me toward him. "Yes, good job," Ethan said. "I think it'd be best to get some fresh air and get away for a bit. Let my friend calm down."

Gustaaf nodded.

I tried to look around him to make sure Vance was alright. I hoped I didn't hurt him too badly.

The Wyranth had him on his back, and one slapped him softly in the face. Vance awoke, startled. "Wh-where am I?"

"In the tavern. You had too much to drink. Let's get back to the barracks," one of the other soldiers said.

Ethan tugged on my arm, forcing me toward the door and away from Vance. The Wyranth didn't spot me. He might not have even remembered the fight, given how drunk he was.

Soon, we were outside in the brisk night air of springtime. I was warm enough from fighting.

"You're attracting too much attention," Ethan said.

"I didn't do anything!" What was he saying? I'd just been sitting there, and Vance came after me. I wanted to wring Ethan's neck.

"It doesn't matter. Notice he didn't come after me. You have to blend in more, be like a tapestry on the wall. Something no one notices because it's just there," Ethan said, leading me away from the tavern and down the main road.

"It wasn't my fault," I maintained, pouting. I didn't care whether I convinced him or not, I just wanted the last word.

The road darkened as we passed the gas lamps that lit the streets near the city. My eyes adjusted, but the trees still obscured so much. Each step required careful consideration, ensuring I didn't trip on a big pebble in the road. I wished Ethan would slow down.

Ethan sighed. "I know it's not your fault, but there's still a way you need to carry yourself on missions like this."

"I don't follow."

"I told you about the tapestry on the wall, right? Something that's just there. Think about the trees alongside the road right now. Are you picking any of them out individually?"

"No, I guess not," I said.

"It's because they're bland. They all look the same. That's what you need to be when you're doing espionage."

"How many missions like this have you been on?"

Ethan paused, mouthing to himself as he counted. "This is my sixth."

And he'd survived all of them. I shouldn't get mad at him. He was trying to teach me something. It still unsettled me. "Where are we going, anyway?"

"We're going to find Dr. Metzengerstein's lab."

"In the middle of the night?" I couldn't see anything. How could we expect to find it?

"It's the only way to hunt around without being seen. Don't worry, we have a general location. Loveridge isn't that big," Ethan said.

We continued down the road. Clouds obscured the moon, leaving us in even greater darkness.

CHAPTER 7

THE ROAD TOOK US TO A PATCH OF LAND WHERE THE FOREST THINNED, revealing a small dirt path leading away from the main road. Tall crops of corn obscured much of the view in the area, but a structure lay beyond. A light was on inside a small wooden home. Next to it stood a taller structure—a barn much like my parents used to have back in Plainsroad Village.

Ethan turned for the path, but I grabbed him by the arm to stop him.

"What are you doing?" he asked in a low tone.

"There's someone inside. A light's on. Shouldn't we sneak through the cornfields?" I pointed to the rows of corn, which could obscure our approach.

"Wouldn't it be more suspicious if someone caught us sneaking around?" Ethan said. "We're Wyranth soldiers, *Klaus*. Act naturally. You do remember the good corporal sending us on patrol, yeah?"

His plan made sense. I bit my lip, annoyed that I didn't think the way he did. There had been a reason he'd gotten a promotion to full knight while I was still a journeyman. I shouldn't be frustrated with myself. This was a learning experience. "Yeah," I said.

"Then let's not delay. We have a lot of ground to cover tonight,"

Ethan said. He shook off my grip from his shoulder and proceeded down the path.

I jogged to catch up with him, and soon found we were at the farm.

The house looked like it was newly constructed—at least much fresher a build than the other structures in Loveridge. Lieutenant Ral had mentioned the farm had burned down when he was here last, but that had been more than two years ago.

Dr. Metzengerstein must have had the place rebuilt. I wondered why he built his lab in Loveridge, but then, it was a small town out of the way. His experiments could go unnoticed here. Besides, Harker-pal, Rislandia's great engineer, had lived here for a long time before the airship *Liliana* returned to the skies. Perhaps a community of scientists had all gathered here.

Ethan wasted no time surveying the scenery. As much as I wanted to get a lay of the land, I understood we didn't want to act like anything was out of the ordinary. I followed his lead as we approached the front porch step of the house.

A little gas lamp hung over the step, lighting the area. The house was painted brown, with white trim around the doorway. A small oval window gave a glimpse inside, obscured by curtains, but with a crack between them where I could see the main light was not on in the entryway.

At first, I thought Ethan was going to push his way inside, but he gave three hard knocks to the door instead, stepping back and waiting patiently. Footsteps sounded on the hard floor inside.

The door opened with a *creak* to reveal an older man with a pointed white beard. He wore a Wyranth uniform, but with no helmet, his balding head shining under the light of the gas lamp. "What're you doing here?" he asked curtly.

"We're patrolling the area on orders of Corporal Gustaaf," Ethan said. "May we come in and inspect the property?"

"Inspect?" the older man asked.

"Yes," Ethan said, not missing a beat. "The Rislandians are gaining ground to the north, and the corporal wishes to make sure everything is in order so we can be ready for an attack."

The man huffed. "If there were an attack here, I would be fleeing back to the capital." He sounded as if we should know that.

Ethan glanced at me. I didn't know what to say and hoped he would continue to lead. He turned his attention back to the man. "Orders are orders," he said, shrugging.

"Come inside. Let me see your papers," the man said. He turned his back on us.

My first instinct was to attack. We had an opening, and it wouldn't be hard to take this man down, as much older than us as he was. And he wasn't nearly as fit-appearing as the two of us, either. The Wyranth didn't seem to have their best about Loveridge, judging from their appearances so far.

But Ethan didn't make any move to try to tackle him. He followed the Wyranth inside. I made my way in after Ethan.

"Shut the door behind you," the man said without looking backward.

I did so. It *creaked* again as it closed.

He led us into a kitchen area, where the light had been on that we'd seen outside. The table looked worn, well used. Several pots and pans hung from hooks on the wall. Another window looked out into the corn fields.

On the Wyranth's table was a book, looking to be a cheap novel of some sort. He also had some food, eaten, bones sitting on a tin plate with a cup beside it. A fly buzzed around the remnants of the meal, picking off what it could. How long it had been there, I couldn't say. It didn't smell bad.

The Wyranth turned around, holding his palm out to Ethan. "Papers."

Ethan reached into his shirt, between the buttons, where he produced the folded papers he'd shown Gustaaf. He handed them to this man.

The Wyranth inspected the letter, mouthing the information as it went along, his forehead wrinkling as he read. "Hans, huh?"

"That's right," Ethan said.

He looked up at me. "And Klaus?"

"Yep," I said.

The Wyranth slammed the papers down on the table, nearly causing me to jump backward. With his other hand, he reached for a pistol holstered at his hip. "These are forgeries. Where did you get them?" he asked.

Ethan saw the move for the weapon and grabbed the man by the arm. The two of them struggled, bumping against the table and knocking the novel off it. I was behind Ethan, unable to do much in the enclosed space to be able to assist him. If Ethan could only turn him around, I'd be able to deliver a hard kick and knock the Wyranth attacker down. I would have offered the advice, but I didn't want to distract him.

"Help!" the Wyranth shouted.

My eyes went wide. It meant there were others here.

"Ethan, we gotta get out of here," I said.

"*Hans*," Ethan growled, still entangled with the Wyranth. He turned and pushed him against the table, which screeched as its legs dragged over tile until the table bumped hard against the wall.

It wasn't a complete opening, but it did allow for me to reach in and grab the Wyranth's pistol from his holster. I pointed it at him. "Enough!" I said.

The Wyranth stopped resisting.

"Shoot him," Ethan said.

Again, I was faced with a situation where he was a helpless man. But this was a war. I needed to take the difficult actions without hesitation. It didn't seem fair, though. We had to have some code of honor. "I..."

The Wyranth tried to scramble away. Ethan delivered an uppercut to his jaw that sent him flying backward. He landed on the table, and it collapsed, making a lot of noise. The Wyranth man's head hit the broken table, and he went limp.

At least it resolved that dilemma.

Ethan looked at me with disappointment. "You can't get skittish now. We've been fighting together for how long?"

"A year, at least."

"And we're in a war. Give me the gun," Ethan said.

I handed it to him.

A noise came from the front of the house. We were out of time. I turned instinctively and winced when I heard the *bang*. I couldn't look down at the man.

It made sense why Ethan did it. He couldn't have him waking up and telling everyone Ethan's real name, our descriptions, or sending everyone on a manhunt for us, but at the same time, I felt there had to be some other way.

"We have to get out of here," Ethan said. "We'll come back later."

He moved for the window and pried it open. It was a small opening, but he was able to get through. I wiggled into the space afterward.

As I did, Wyranth soldiers bounded into the kitchen. They shouted, more occupied with the man we had killed than us for the time being.

I scrambled to the ground, stopping to look at Ethan for orders.

"Go!" Ethan said.

We bolted for the corn fields. Gunshots rang out behind us. I didn't dare look back for fear it would slow me down. If a bullet were going to strike me, I couldn't do much about it. Staying on the move was the best way to make getting hit a less likely possibility.

We pushed into the corn fields. Some of the clouds had retreated, and moon lit the area well enough, but we could hide between the stalks with ease. There would most certainly be a search party for us, and they'd be coming soon.

Ethan kept running hard, apparently not satisfied with the crops as cover. He headed for the forest beyond. The trees would work even better and obscure us from the moonlight.

I hoped it would be enough. All I wanted was to get out of here and back to Rislandian-controlled territory. Despite how bored it used to make me, I suddenly found myself longing for guard duty.

CHAPTER 8

IT WAS MUCH EASIER TO NAVIGATE THE DARK OF NIGHT IN THE FIELDS than in the forest. Once in the thick of the trees, I found myself nearly running into bushes or tripping over roots every few steps. The leaves obscured the moon and stars, which made the area almost pitch black. Even though my eyes had long-since adjusted, I could barely see.

Ethan didn't seem to have as much problem as I did. He kept rushing ahead. He had to, otherwise the Wyranth were sure to catch up. They'd be sending a search party out soon enough.

We pushed deep into the forest. My legs ached by the time we slowed our pace. We'd been doing a lot of walking and running the last day, and we weren't likely to get any rest tonight.

"What do we do?" I asked in a low tone. "Do we head back?"

Ethan didn't answer me, but, instead, reached into his jacket, from where he revealed an egg-shaped, metal device with clockwork components. He unclipped it from a strap.

"What's that?"

"It's called a grenade," Ethan said. "Our scientists reverse engineered the exploding bags we encountered on the Zenwey continent and came up with something a little more elegant." He pointed to the gears atop it. "The grenade explodes on a timer. I pull a pin out from the top, twist the clockwork, and it detonates after the gears wind down."

"Pretty useful," I said, trying to conceal my jealousy that I didn't get the new explosive for the mission.

"It is. And I think it will be handy in this situation." Ethan inclined his head as if trying to listen. "We'll hear the Wyranth coming. When we do, we can draw them toward a place where we drop the grenade and take them out before they see us."

It sounded like a decent plan, though very dependent on Ethan's timing with the clockwork. Did he know how fast the gears turned before they exploded?

"Alright," I said.

We waited in silence. Every sound coming from the forest made me jumpy. A few crackles sounded like footsteps, but it was just a squirrel. Another rustling turned out to a bird flapping its wings, which eventually squawked to reveal itself. Too much time passed. Had the Wyranth abandoned us?

Suddenly, Ethan perked. He held a finger up to me to signal that I should be quiet.

We waited in silence. Every time something stirred in the forest, both of us jumped. We dared not laugh at each other for our unease, in case our voices echoed in the forest and someone heard us.

Ethan paced the area around where I held still. If the Wyranth were going to come after us, surely they would have by now, wouldn't they? I didn't want to question Ethan because he tended to get so cranky when I did, but I also didn't want us to waste time.

If this didn't work, we would in all likelihood return to Rislandia City empty-handed. The Wyranth probably knew our faces, and we would be well-known.

And Ethan would probably blame me for the mission's failure. As if it would somehow be my fault for us getting spotted by the Wyranth officer in the house. Ethan had already chastised me for drawing too much attention in the tavern, even though it hadn't been my fault.

I was still curious as to how the Wyranth soldier had spotted the forged documents. Not that I was an expert in Wyranth military papers by any means, but Gustaaf hadn't questioned them. It must have taken a keen eye to determine we were fakes.

Leaves rustled, pulling me from my thoughts. Ethan perked.

More noises came from the distance, and then I spotted the silhouettes of men. They had to be Wyranth. Who else would be out in the forest at this hour?

Ethan seemed to come to the same conclusion. He held his grenade up, twisting the clockwork contraption on it, so it began to tick down. He looked at me. Then he surprised me

"Hey, James!" he shouted. "I think we've finally lost them."

"What are you doing?" I said through my teeth in a low tone.

"Good thing!" Ethan said cheerily. His voice echoed in the forest.

The rumbling increased. The Wyranth were going to be hot on our heels for sure now. "This way!" one of them shouted.

Ethan pulled the pin for the grenade and chucked it in the direction of the voice.

He took off running. I finally understood his plan and tried to catch up with him. We needed to draw the Wyranth in to where we dropped the grenade.

Lights shone. They were dim, the kind I'd often seen from handheld gas lamps. I glanced over my shoulder to spot three soldiers approaching us. They held their gas lamps in one hand, guns in the other.

Ethan tugged me by the arm, pulling me behind a tree.

I grunted by instinct. Ethan held a finger to his lips.

The Wyranth hadn't given any indication they'd spotted us yet, still searching the area. Ethan drew his pistol and pointed toward them.

He fired, the shot ringing out.

The Wyranth stopped moving forward, while shouting at each other and looking for cover. They'd be on top of us at any moment.

I had my back to a wide tree, which both Ethan and I kept between them and us. Ethan kept his focus on the soldiers, gun pointed toward them. I wasn't in much of a position to help.

The grenade went off.

The blast rattled the forest around us, branches shaking and leaves falling from the trees.

I turned around to try to get a look, peeking around the tree but not exposing myself too much. A gas lamp was knocked over on the ground, the foliage around it catching fire. A body lay beside it. From the light of the flame, I could see one Wyranth scrambling away. I couldn't tell what happened to the third soldier. My mind wandered, and I imagined a very painful demise.

But I couldn't fret for him. There was still one enemy left out there.

Ethan fired another shot. The bullet slammed into a tree, bark blasting into the air. The small fire gave us an advantage because we could see the area where the Wyranth hid. He'd set his gas lamp down, further illuminating his position. He was hidden behind the tree where Ethan stood. His shadow grew long across the area in front of me, cast from the soft light.

He leaned around to try to get to us, his pointed helmet shining from the flickering of the fire—a perfect target.

I raised my gun and fired.

The shot rang out. The Wyranth spun, collapsing to the ground. I'd hit him!

Ethan came out from his cover, cocking his head to survey the scene. "About time you pulled your weight around here," he said.

"Hey," I said, unable to come up with a good retort.

We moved over to the bodies of the Wyranth. Ethan bent over and took the jacket off one of them. He held it out and smothered the small fire with it. Smoke rose, causing Ethan to cough a few times. He glanced at me. "Can't well let the forest burn down. We want Loveridge to be intact when we take it back."

"True," I said, scanning the bodies. How many more Wyranth knew we were out here?

It'd been a tough few hours. I didn't know what overcame me or why I'd been so hesitant to fight the enemy. It was as if I had some block in my mind I couldn't get over, ever since returning to Plainsroad Village, the place where my parents had died. The stresses of this war were getting to me. I almost couldn't remember a time without fighting.

Ethan turned, leaving the Wyranth where we left them. "Come on," he said, trudging back the way we'd come.

"Where are we going?" I asked.

"To the farm."

"Now?"

"Yeah, most of the guards have to be cleared out by now. This is it. If we wait 'til sunrise, we'll never be able to get what we came for." He motioned for me to follow. "Come on."

CHAPTER 9

WE HADN'T SPENT TOO LONG HIDING IN THE FOREST. I CHECKED MY
pocket watch in the light of the moon, and it was still around the two
o'clock hour. We had a few hours yet until sunrise.

The lights in the house were off. It appeared as if Ethan's instincts
were correct. We'd cleared the house of the Wyranth by getting them
to follow us.

The walk to Dr. Metzengerstein's residence proved uneventful,
though I kept my hands on my gun all the same. My palms sweated. I
expected Wyranth soldiers to pop out of the fields at any moment and
start firing at us.

None came.

Ethan didn't knock this time, walking causally to the front door. It
was locked. He raised his leg and kicked the door hard.

With a *crack*, the door burst open, swinging inward and hitting the
wall inside. It made so much noise I turned to make sure no one
behind us heard it. The fields remained empty, a soft wind blowing
through the stalks of corn.

Nothing to worry about.

I took a deep breath as I followed Ethan into the residence.

Where we'd gone straight into a kitchen area last time. This time,

Ethan made for a different door. The interior door was also locked, and Ethan kicked it in, as well. He grinned at me after the door popped open. I think he liked showing off his strength against inanimate objects.

The door opened to reveal tables with beakers, small machines, tools everywhere. A large machine stood against the back wall, with gauges and an exhaust pipe, which protruded through a small hole in the wall. It looked almost like a steam engine, but what could it be doing here?

The engine had a hose coming out the other end attached to a strange device on a tripod. The device had a lever on it, an oblong shaped piece of metal the size of both of my arms put together, with a small point of metal protruding at the end. What could it be for?

"This must be the doctor's lab," Ethan said.

Metzengerstein had a small desk in the corner with some drawers. I slipped past Ethan to the desk and opened it up.

One of the drawers contained papers inside of a folder. I opened the folder and placed them on the desk.

Ethan lit a small gas lamp in the room and set it near the papers. Most of the papers contained mathematical computations I couldn't understand. I'd had a rudimentary education, but there were too many numbers and symbols, and I had no idea what they meant.

I spotted a design of what appeared to be the spidery woman Ral had told us about. I made sure to dog-ear the corner on that, even though I didn't understand the mathematical language below it. Our people would want to analyze that.

Another of the papers had a sketch of the device by us. It had some pulsing energy coming from the device. "This might be a weapon," I said.

"We might want to save those plans, then," Ethan said. He loomed over my shoulder. "Do you see anything that might have to do with airship design?"

I kept thumbing through the papers, and then I shook my head. I came upon some writing. "Wait…" It appeared as if it were a letter.

. . .

Dear Dr. Metzengerstein,

We've completed initial experiments with the power systems you provided us, and we believe we've reached a state where we can produce a prototype of the new mechanized unit.

Your discovery is truly astounding. Though these aren't quite the controllable automatons we'd initially devised, the mechanized units should prove to be a worthy addition to the Iron Emperor's arsenal.

We should have the prototype ready for you by the beginning of the Month of Princes. I hope you'll be able to join us at our facility to see our tests.

Sincerely,

Mr. Stephen Nava.

"This looks interesting," I said.

Ethan frowned, narrowing his eyes at the letter. "Doesn't seem to have to do with an airship, but I'm sure our people will be happy to have information on Wyranth technological developments. We shouldn't linger here, though. Let our intelligence analysts determine what's important. Grab the whole stack and let's get out of here."

As he spoke, the whirring of a steam motor sounded outside. Both of us froze, staring at each other.

A light shone at the house. Even through the dark curtains of the lab, its brightness pierced the window. Would they be able to see our shadows inside?

"We have the house surrounded!" came a familiar voice. It was loud, amplified by some device or another that caused the voice to lose most of its lower tones. "Hans, Klaus—or should I say, James and Ethan—we know you're in there." I recalled hearing the voice before–Gustaaf. He'd no doubt brought his whole team.

How did they know our real names?

Ethan shuffled over to the window, standing beside it. He moved the curtain to take a quick peek, and then looked back at me. For once, he seemed nervous. His eyes scanned the room as if trying to figure out a plan.

I didn't want to interrupt his thought process. He'd always come up with something in the time I'd known him. Wouldn't he do so here?

He was quiet for too long. The Wyranth fired a warning shot outside.

"This is your last chance. Come out with your hands up," Gustaaf said.

"See that bookshelf?" Ethan asked. He pointed to one behind me.

"Yeah," I said.

"Slide it in front of the door. We don't want it to be easy for them to get in here."

I moved to the other side of the shelf and pushed. The heavy wood scraped on the floor, making a painful sound, but it moved. It scratched the floor. The shape of the bookshelf etched in the floorboards where it moved, a spot where the light and dust didn't hit.

I secured it in front of the door and surveyed my handiwork. It would hold for a bit unless something really heavy pushed on the door and knocked it over. At least it would buy us some time.

"Now what do we do?" I asked.

Ethan bit down on his lower lip. He grabbed his pistol from his holster and lifted it upward. "We fight like our lives depend on it," he said.

It wasn't what I wanted to hear, but I didn't expect any less.

CHAPTER 10

ETHAN CREPT TO THE FRONT WALL AGAIN AND PUSHED THE EDGE OF THE curtain over, revealing a checkered paned window with the blinding light shining from beyond it. The shadow of a man with a pointed helmet operated a large crank to keep the light's power going. Its brightness grew and faded along with his cranking.

I stood directly in the path of the light. Ethan tried to motion me aside, but I'd been too busy fretting over our long-term plans to take much notice. How were we going to escape this place if they had us surrounded? The whole Wyranth army could very well know we were here.

Bullets shattered the glass. I ducked and moved to the side, out of the direction of the fire. Several more shots pelted the wall behind where I had been standing. I was lucky nothing connected with me.

"By Malaky, what're you thinking?" Ethan asked.

"Sorry!" I had to get my head in this fight and not worry about the future.

Ethan pointed his gun through the broken glass and returned fire. Men shouted and cursed, but I couldn't see whether he'd hit anything or not. Regardless, he was right. I needed to help.

I slunk up to the other side of the curtains and pushed them to the center. Bullets had poked holes in the window on my side of it, allowing me to extend my arm and fire toward the Wyranth.

I didn't aim for anyone in particular but, instead, pointed my gun toward the big light. The brightness made it difficult for us to see as much as it allowed the enemy to pinpoint us.

I fired.

The light shattered. Whatever material it was made of erupted into a quick flame upward, and then it went dim. I tried my best to get a good look from the window, my eyes readjusting to the darkness.

The light had been attached to the back of a large horseless carriage with a steam stack protruding upward. There were at least four Wyranth standing guard.

Gunshots blasted at our windows again. I leaned off to the side, and Ethan did the same on the other.

"We can't hold out here forever," I said. "We don't have enough bullets."

"I'm aware of that. But I don't have a plan," Ethan said. "Do you have any ideas?"

He wasn't patronizing. The question was genuine. Ethan needed my help.

Proud of the fact, I stood a little straighter. We had our small guns. The Wyranth claimed to have us surrounded. What could we do? It would be better to get the Wyranth inside for some close combat. Then we could use our swords. But if they got in, it would only be a matter of time before one shot us.

We had to get the plans I'd found out of here somehow. Our kingdom needed to know of the threats being developed by the Wyranth, even if I didn't understand all of the pages I read.

The plans. I glanced back to the folder of papers I'd dropped to the ground in my haste, and then got to my knees in front of them. Maybe there was something we could use.

Ethan exchanged volleys with the Wyranth and reloaded his gun. "What are you doing?" he asked.

"Seeing if there's anything in here we can use," I said.

I thumbed through the pages again, pausing at the letter regarding the mechanized units. Looking up, I saw nothing in the lab that could be construed as such. Useless. I resumed my search.

Bullets fired from outside. Ethan returned fire. "What about the big machine in the corner? It looks a little like a gun."

"We have no idea what it does," I said. "I'm trying to find out."

"If we don't do something soon, I'm going to be out of bullets." He turned to reload.

I bit my lip. Rummaging through a mad scientist's notes wasn't going to get anything done. This whole trip I'd been too slow, unable to act when required. I'd thought going on a spy reconnaissance mission would be fun, but after everything I'd seen so far, maybe I wasn't cut out for this.

No, that couldn't be it.

I was a Knight of the Crystal Spire, promoted to journeyman faster than nearly anyone on record. The kingdom counted on me, regardless of any guilt or squeamishness I might feel. Ethan had the right of it. I set the notes down and pushed myself off the floor. "You're right," I said. "We can't worry about it. We have to try."

"Figure it out, quick. This is my last magazine," Ethan said.

This was my moment. I had to act, and I couldn't worry any longer. Being in Plainsroad Village had shaken me, but it was up to me to rise up and make sure we got this information back to our people to decipher. Ethan didn't really have a plan here, but I could make a difference. How though? I bit my lip, trying to think.

I jogged over to the wall with the furnace. It had to power the device somehow. But how did this turn on?

There didn't appear to be a keyhole like horseless carriages often had. The airship engine ignited aether fuel, but I hadn't been down in the engine room when the ship started. I found myself wishing I'd listened more to the prattling stories of the *Liliana's* chief engineer, Harkerpal, when I'd had the time.

I opened the furnace door. Coals rested inside.

The Wyranth pushed to enter. Their efforts bumped the door

against the bookcase. Things were about to get a whole lot worse if the Wyranth managed to get past our makeshift barrier.

"Hurry!" Ethan shouted.

"I'm trying," I said.

I scanned the room again. There was a can with a small funnel protruding from it. I picked it up. It was heavy, and liquid swayed from side to side in it. I brought the can to my face so I could sniff and see if it was just water or something else. The smell was poignant, almost burning my nostrils. Definitely not water. Fuel?

Whether the can held fuel or not, I had to try.

I poured some of the liquid over the coals in the furnace until they became wet. Part of my apprentice training involved starting fires, basic survival skills. We'd done a little bit of camping outside the city. I needed some sticks, something to rub together to get a spark, and all of it would take off. I could use the legs of the desk in here, but breaking them off would take time.

Then I recalled bullets sometimes sparked when they hit metal. I could fire inside it and start it up that way. I stepped back, nearly to the bookcase. There was no telling how big the fire would be if it did start.

The case rumbled against my back as the Wyranth continued to push. They fired bullets into the door, and I heard wood snapping and crackling behind me. Fortunately, they hadn't shot a hole through the case yet.

I leveled my gun at the furnace and fired into it.

Nothing happened.

Had I done something wrong?

I tried again. Still no flame.

"What, by Malaky, are you doing over there?" Ethan said through clenched teeth.

"Don't worry about it. I've got this," I said.

This had to work. I narrowed my eyes in focus, aiming directly for the coals, and then I pulled the trigger a third time.

The bullet *clanged*, and the coals burst into flames. The light was bright from it, and even from across the room, a wave of heat came across my face. Flames erupted from the furnace, but they died back, settling into a small fire inside. The engine started up. Gears rotated, groaning as they turned. A belt made a scratching noise, and exhaust hissed out the steam stack. It worked.

Now to find out what this contraption was good for.

I grabbed the tripod. The thing was heavier than I thought it would be, but I could feel the energy pulsing through the tube. A lot of it. The device was heating up. I wouldn't be able to carry it for long.

Ethan helped me to place it in front of the window, not straight on but slightly to the side so it wouldn't become an easy target for the Wyranth. We got it in place, and I moved to a position where I could point the protruding center outward, hoping this was the direction it was supposed to go.

"Move," Ethan said.

"No way. You always get to use the new devices. Besides, this is my plan," I said.

"You used the auto-electrocuter last time."

"You had the grenade. I didn't even know those existed."

Ethan frowned.

Before we could argue further, the bookcase came crashing down.

It narrowly missed where we were standing, hitting the floor with a loud *thud*. Two Wyranth soldiers pushed through the door.

Ethan already had his gun drawn, and he fired on one of them, connecting.

The soldier collapsed. The other took cover behind the door frame. We had lost our meager defenses.

The second Wyranth pointed his gun inside and fired blindly. A bullet ricocheted off the big machine on the wall.

I pointed to the wall. "Keep them occupied. I'll handle the ones outside."

Ethan nodded.

I couldn't believe he'd listened to me, but I didn't have time to reflect on it. I returned my focus to the device. It had a long trigger on the bottom of it, just like a rifle. Whatever this device did, it was about to get interesting.

I pushed the curtains open wider, exposing myself to the Wyranth outside, but gaining a good view of my targets.

The Wyranth behind the door fired another shot. Ethan rushed the door. I couldn't afford to look back, not while staring down Wyranth of my own. A *thump* sounded against the side wall, rattling the house. Someone groaned, but I kept my eyes forward.

I pulled the trigger and held it down.

The machine *whirred.* The engine rattled. Even more hot energy came through the tube. Sweat dripped down my face just from standing by it. Fortunately, the energy didn't conduct to the trigger.

The face of the device pulsed, blue light swelling in it. And then a beam of energy shot outward, more intense than anything I'd ever seen before.

The energy hit the Wyranth horseless carriage first. It shattered the front of it as if the metal vehicle were made from glass. The carriage flipped in the air, then crashed below. The Wyranth soldiers tried to dive out of the way, but I turned the beam to hit one of them.

I pivoted the device back and forth, casting a wide array of the energy out. Dirt, plants, rocks, everything flew in the air as the beam tore the earth apart in front of the house.

I managed to hit every Wyranth in sight. The amount of power I wielded was incredible. My plan had worked.

For the first time in my life, I felt like a real leader. I deserved to be a knight.

But it was getting hotter in the room.

The engine started making strange noises, puttering and pattering in odd rhythms.

I looked behind me. Ethan rushed back through the doorway. "James! Get out of here. That thing's gonna blow!"

"Huh?" I asked.

The engine had turned red hot. Smoke seeped through the pipes and clouded the room. I'd been so intent on the battle I hadn't noticed.

I let go of the trigger and ran for the door. Remembering the reason we came, I stopped in my tracks, bending over to pick up the binder before continuing onward. We moved into the hallway and back toward the kitchen where we'd first come in. A Wyranth soldier lay crumpled in the hallway, where Ethan must have dispatched him just prior.

We hopped over the Wyranth and made our way into the kitchen. Ethan opened the window, and we jumped outside.

CHAPTER 11

I DROPPED TO THE GROUND, BENDING MY KNEES AS I HIT. DUST KICKED up around my feet.

Ethan had already taken off running. There were no Wyranth in sight on this side of the house. The ones who had surrounded us—if the Wyranth had been telling the truth—must have either come inside or gone back around front to see what the commotion was.

The house exploded.

A concussive force knocked me through the air, sending me flying head first into the dirt.

I'd been involved in airship battles with exploding shells coming very close to tearing us to pieces, but that was one of the largest blasts I'd ever encountered. It tore the house apart, the exterior walls lurching and swaying before collapsing.

A wave of fire roared from the window. The flames singed the back of my neck. It was hot, but I didn't burn.

Shouting came from the opposite side of the house. I could hardly hear through my ears ringing from the explosion. Whatever was being said, it was lost on me.

I clutched the folder tightly, pulled myself to my feet, and scrambled forward.

Glancing back at the house, I saw the level of destruction the machine's overload had caused. The whole roof had been blown to bits, the wind carrying them the opposite direction. Where once stood a building now lay rubble. Smoke shot skyward, obscuring my view.

There wasn't time to stop. I scrambled to my feet and ran after Ethan, who already ran a good ten paces ahead of me.

We ran through the corn fields and back toward the forest. This time, we had to get out with our lives.

Ethan led the way and didn't wait for me. I pushed my legs harder to try to keep up with him.

Gunshots blasted behind me. I instinctively slowed.

"Keep going!" Ethan shouted without looking back.

I came back up to speed, not questioning his orders. There was a time to argue, but now wasn't one of them. We would be overwhelmed by Wyranth if they caught us. They probably had the whole of their contingent in Loveridge coming after us.

A few more shots echoed in the forest, but they seemed to become more distant. Whether we outran them, or the Wyranth gave up, I couldn't tell. I didn't dare look back, lest I trip or slow myself down some other way. Moving was a good way to make oneself a more difficult target to hit.

My lungs burned. I had inhaled a little bit of the smoke from the blast and, combined with the exertion, it was making it difficult to breathe. My legs felt like mush. We'd been going too hard with very little break. Though I'd spent a lot of time running up and down the steps of the giant Crystal Spire in Rislandia City in training, running this hard proved to be a much greater endurance test.

My tenacity here meant life or death, however. If I stopped, the Wyranth could catch up. Ethan wouldn't slow down until it was safe. I had to follow his lead.

Our hard run through the forest seemed to go on forever. After a while, I wondered if Ethan even knew which way we were headed. I hadn't checked my bearings, and with the thick tree cover of the forest, it was difficult to get a good view of the moon and stars while moving at this pace.

Finally, when my legs felt as if they were about to give way, Ethan slowed down. He turned back to me, breathing just as heavily as I was, sweat dripping down his face. His hair was clumped together, dirty and sweaty. We must have looked like wrecks. "You doing okay?" he asked between hard breaths.

"Yeah," I managed to say.

Speaking made me realize how dry my mouth was. I wished we hadn't dropped our packs in the house the first time we'd run from the Wyranth. A canteen would have been wonderful.

"Good," Ethan said. "We shouldn't stop completely. The Wyranth might be coming for us still, or we might run into one of those rabid packs of roving soldiers in their serum-withdrawal delirium. We're going to have to press on until we get back to Rislandian territory."

I nodded.

He seemed content with my gesture, turning back and pressing forward. He walked instead of running now, but we'd been going for so long my legs wanted to give way.

The sky was pink on the horizon between the trees. The sun was making its way up. We'd run through the night. Judging from the sun's location, we were heading north, which was good. We would reach Rislandian territory soon enough.

My adrenaline slowly wore off, and fatigue set in. Even more than my lungs and my legs, my eyes grew weary. I could hardly keep them open. And they were dry. Everything irritated me. I just wanted to collapse in a bed. I'd even settle for the forest floor for a little nap.

But sleep wouldn't be in the cards. Our lives still depended on us moving forward.

This was by far the worst mission I'd been on, including the time I'd been captured to become a gladiator. At least then I had water and food and rest when I needed it. None of the other battles so far had taxed me like this. But this is what I signed up for. This was what knights had to endure for the safety and security of everyone else.

The forest began to thin. We had to be closer to Greenhorne or Plainsroad Village at this point. Either way, our army would be close by.

We reached a flat area. I used the opportunity to rest my eyes even as I moved forward. There wasn't anything to trip on here.

Moments later, I found myself stumbling forward. I had fallen asleep while walking. I laughed at myself, unable to believe I'd done such a thing.

"Something funny?" Ethan asked.

"Nah, just too tired," I said.

"I know the feeling."

My feet dragged. Each step became harder. We had to reach one of our towns soon. All I wanted was rest and water. I'd give anything for them.

Shadowed figures appeared in the distance. It was still barely twilight, and I couldn't make out who was in front of us. Ethan was at the ready, his gun pointed. Hadn't he run out of ammunition? Perhaps he would be able to bluff our way out of a confrontation, but with how aggressive the Wyranth were, I doubted it.

Rifles cocked. Bullets flew toward us. Ethan ducked.

"Hold your fire!" he shouted. He put his hands up, pistol in the air. "We're not here to fight."

The men firing on us came forward, they kept their guns trained, though they stopped shooting. There were six of them in total. When they came close, I spotted the dark gray uniforms of the Grand Rislandian Army, along with the brass Crest of Malaky over their breast pockets—a gear with angel wings on the side, and a crown atop it. They wore matching caps with the same insignia embroidered on them. They didn't look pleased to see us.

"We're Rislandian, too," Ethan assured them.

"Yeah?" one of the infantrymen asked, a man with hard eyes and a well-trimmed beard. "Why are you wearing Wyranth uniforms?"

"Intelligence," Ethan said. "We're knights."

The Rislandians grumbled to themselves. "We're gonna have to take you to our commander to verify you."

"Of course," Ethan said.

I sighed in relief. Even though they were suspicious of us, we were back among our people. It would all be over soon.

The infantrymen still gave us a complete run through. They took our weapons and patted us down. Ethan said we were lucky they didn't bind us. Eventually, they led us to their camp.

EPILOGUE

CID TURNED OVER ONE OF THE PIECES OF PAPER I'D BROUGHT HIM. HE'D listened to our whole story before getting into the actual documents we'd recovered and wrinkled his forehead as he delved into what we found.

I glanced at Ethan. He seemed focused on Cid.

We waited as Cid quietly flipped through the pages. I was getting impatient. It'd been three full days since we'd been back, and I hadn't been able to see Princess Reina. The palace was closed off to visitors, and they made no exceptions. It was all so strange.

"Hmm," Cid said.

I wasn't sure if I should open my mouth and ask Cid what he was thinking. My eyes shifted to Ethan again, hoping he would take the lead, but he said nothing.

Cid looked back up at us. "This confirms Ral's reports on the strange spider-like woman he saw. I didn't mention this in front of him, but a good number of the army brass thought he had been shell-shocked from battle. Now he has proof he wasn't seeing things. Still, it's a shame you didn't find any information pertaining to airships. Latest reports are that there have been some struggles in the rebuilding effort."

"They can't piece the *Liliana* back together?" I asked.

"From my understanding, the ship is mostly reconstructed, but there is an element to the engine that's not allowing it to lift off as it did before. Our scientists are baffled because it looks the same." Cid straightened the papers and placed them all into one stack.

"Who created the airship engines?" Ethan asked.

"A man by the name of Dr. Lawrence du Brass. I'm afraid he's long since passed. He was one of the first targets of our original war against the Wyranth years ago. Harkerpal has done all he can, and he learned a lot about the airship design since then, but there's something missing. It takes a lot for such a wooden monstrosity to take to the skies. Ah, well, it's not a concern we can do much about now," Cid said.

He extended his hand to me, and then Ethan. We shook hands as he stood. "You gentlemen did a great job recovering what you could from Dr. Metzengerstein's lab. You're to be commended."

"Thank you, sir," Ethan said.

I nodded.

"I know the army's intelligence division will be eager to get their hands on the information here. There's so much to go through, it might lead to many developments in our armaments and technologies. I'm especially interested in these mechanized units. I'm sure others will be as well. If these end up in Wyranth hands—"

"We'll have to ensure it doesn't happen," Ethan said, smiling at Cid. "James and I would be happy to volunteer for a mission to Nyanzi to see what's going on, if you need anyone."

I perked a little in my chair. Mechanized units and seeing a whole new country? This sounded like a great job for a knight, though I hoped it wouldn't involve going undercover again. On the other hand, it meant I'd be further away from the princess. Would my missions always take me away from her? There had to be a way to balance being a knight with a life.

Ethan glanced at me as if looking for backup, but I said nothing.

"You two will be the first I'll suggest once we get to that point," Cid said. "For now, we have a lot of work to do to set up supply lines to cities we've recaptured. I'll need you two to escort a group of civilians to Plainsroad Village to get them situated for farming. Without food production for the next year, there won't be much left to talk about." He stood. "Now, if you'll excuse me, I should report to the High Knight and the palace staff."

I wished I could go with him. I wanted to see Reina more than anything. Even though I'd only been gone a couple of days, it felt like an eternity since I'd been in her presence.

"C'mon, James," Ethan said. "We'll be ready when you need us." He pushed his chair back, stood, and headed for the door.

I followed Ethan out, back into the courtyard. We'd won. Our mission had been successful. By all rights, we had a victory. Cid even said we should be commended. Why did it feel so hollow?

It was because of what we'd found, or failed to find, I surmised. We'd hoped to recover airship plans or information on genetic testing, to get them out of Wyranth hands, and to assist with the rebuilding effort. We found some information, but there should have been more. There should have been a way to end this war.

Unfortunately, life didn't always hand easy answers. We would have to keep fighting.

I slumped my shoulders as I walked. It hit me how tired I was. It would be nice to be back in the barracks again. The bed was familiar, even if I had to sleep in a room with three other boys, one of whom snored loudly.

A shadow fell over me, the figure of a woman. As I looked up, I recognized her scraggly, dirty-blonde hair and bright eyes. She wore her signature brown skirt and a white blouse, with a red cape flowing behind her—Zaira von Monocle.

She floated right past me and pounced on Ethan, wrapping her arms around him.

He kissed her on the cheek, holding her off the ground. His face lit up with excitement, and he whirled her around.

Zaira gave a dim smile as he set her down. Something was different about her. She didn't quite have the energy she usually did. "I'm glad you're back," Zaira said.

"Glad to be back," Ethan said.

"Hey, Zair-bear," I said.

Zaira gave me a weak smile. "Welcome back, James."

"What's been happening here in Rislandia City?" I asked.

Zaira dropped her smile in short order. Everything these days served as a reminder of what we'd lost. Even though Zaira didn't say that's what she was feeling, I knew her well enough to be able to read her expressions. "A lot of waiting, to be honest. I want to get back out in the airship again. I'm going land crazy."

"Land crazy?" Ethan chuckled.

"It's real. My father said he used to feel the same way when he was stuck dirtside," Zaira said.

"Do you know why the palace is sealed off? Everyone's acting so strange," I said.

Zaira grimaced. "I don't know how much I'm supposed to say."

"You can trust us," Ethan said.

Zaira sighed. "Okay. Don't tell anyone else. The king's health has taken a turn for the worse. No one's sure what's going on. I wasn't given specifics, and I don't think anyone's supposed to know. They've brought in a specialist to see to him." She shrugged. "I'm sure he'll be fine. The stress probably got to him."

"Probably," Ethan said. "I know sometimes it's made me feel ill."

"I hope he'll recover soon," I said.

Ethan and Zaira's eyes met each other's. There was a fire and intensity to their gazes, and I felt awkward standing there. I needed to get away.

"I should say hello to my bunkmates. I'll let you two catch up," I said.

"Good to see you, James," Zaira said.

I hurried away from the two lovebirds. It wasn't as if their displays of affection offended me. Reina and I were just as bad, but it wasn't fun to stand by and watch the two of them.

Fun. I wished I could have simple, innocent fun like I used to. Everything seemed so heavy all the time these days. The stones in the courtyard seemed darker than before, older, lifeless. It might have been my imagination, but it was like the Wyranth had sapped the joy out of Rislandia City itself.

I'd come here to become a knight, and I was on my way. No one else around me had been promoted to journeyman so quickly. I'd make it to full knight in this next year, I was sure of that. But I had to remember the reason I wanted to be one. It was for my king, for my country, and to show the world I was the best Rislandia had to offer.

I opened my hand, realizing I'd been clenching my fist as I walked. There was still a lot of work to do before we could get everything back to normal. I would be up to the task, whatever it took.

NEXT IN THE SERIES...

If you enjoyed this book, please leave a review on Amazon.
   Coming in 2020!
   Zaira's adventures will continue in *Attack of the Nightmen*!
   Join Jon's mailing list for updates on new releases.

RISLANDIAN TIMELINE

23rd Year of King Malaky XV Reign – 20 years before the events of *For Steam And Country*, Baron Theodore von Monocle flies his ship on its first mission to Tyndree on the east coast of Rislandia between Wyranth at High Mesa Castle. He rescued duchess named Liliana, fell in love, and named his airship for her.

24nd Year of King Malaky XV's Reign – The *Liliana* travels to the One-Eyed King's domain on the Ebony Sands Coast. Theodore convinced the king he'd work for him as a mercenary, was imprisoned in the ruse, and escaped with the help of his crew. Theodore returns to Rislandia and marries Liliana.

25th year of King Malaky XV's Reign – King Malaky XV is assassinated by Wyranth. A new airship is commissioned. A big battle occurs, and an uneasy peace is achieved.

1st Year of King Malaky XVI's Reign – Von Monocle takes the *Liliana* on an exploratory world tour. The new king wants trade relations and peace, a new positive outlook for the world.

2nd Year King Malaky XVI's Reign – On a 2nd exploratory tour, the *Liliana* travels to the Sands of Zarma, where they find a treasure chest and the crew had a strange disease. The Tyndree Kingdom folds into the Wyranth Empire.

3rd Year of King Malaky XVI's Reign – Zaira is born. The Atreblan

Kingdom sends an expedition around the world to find treasure, and comes back with a supply of aether-fuel ("Black Gold"). The Rislandians desperately need the fuel for their airship fleet, and seek trade. Theodore von Monocle agrees to go to the Island of the Fae to help an Atreblan noble in exchange for fuel ("Baron von Monocle and the Island of the Fae").

5th Year King Malaky XVI's Reign (Zaira is 2) – 3rd expedition across the world. Trade negotiations with the Tribes of Zenway. Theodore comes across a book given by a shaman attached to chief, she told that the Areth continent didn't have a grasp of true history, the settlers a thousand years ago had forgotten much. The book had legends about giants who roamed the land in ancient times.

6th Year of King Malaky XVI's Reign (Zaira is 3) – Small skirmishes occur with the Wyranth at the border, frightening the Rislandian people. The Airship takes a number of casualties, grating on the crew. Baron von Monocle turns to a young chef's assistant, Talyen von Cravat, to come up with an idea to help the crew's morale ("The Battlecry Of The *Liliana*")

7th Year King Malaky XVI's Reign (Zaira is 4) – Twin Tops Mountains rescue mission in winter (during the month of fools) to save starving dying people.

8th Year of King Malaky XVI'S Reign (Zaira is 5) – Baron von Monocle travels to the Dragonmist Isles to retrieve a rare flower for his anniversary with his wife.

15th Year of King Malaky XVI's Reign (Zaira is 12) – Wyranth are getting aggressive again after a period of relative peace. Portsgate floods after a recent hurricane. Zaira's mother Liliana dies while Theo's away fighting. 1st battle at Border River.

16ᵗʰ Year of King Malaky XVI's Reign (Zaira is 13) – The 2ⁿᵈ Wyranth War begins.

17ᵗʰ Year of King Malaky XVI's Reign (Zaira is 14) – The 2ⁿᵈ Battle of the Border River. Baron Theodore von Monocle goes missing. Commander Von Cravat leads a counter assault 9 days later. Afterward, von Cravat can't handle the loss of the Baron and grounds the ship in Loveridge ("Tangled Web").

18ᵗʰ Year of King Malaky XVI's Reign (Zaira is 15) – Captain Von Cravat tries to get the crew back together and fails.

19ᵗʰ Year of King Malaky XVI's Reign (Zaira is 16) – Zaira von Monocle inherits her father's airship and mounts a mission to rescue her father based on rumors he may still be alive (*For Steam And Country*). James Gentry is trained as a Knight and uncovers a Wyranth plot ("Knight Training"). Zaira takes the airship to the Zenwey Continent in hopes of finding more giant's blood to help cure the Wyranth soldiers of their addictions (*The Blood Of Giants*). When she returns, she finds the Wyranth have invaded and she must save her kingdom (*The Fight For Rislandia*). James Gentry is sent to guard King Malaky and Princess Reina at their retreat ("Guard Training").

20ᵗʰ Year of King Malaky XVI's Reign (Zaira is 17) – The knights play a prank on James Gentry ("Hazing"). James and Ethan go on a mission into Wyranth occupied territory ("Spy Training"). Zaira is faced with a difficult choice to bring peace to Rislandia. (*The Iron Wedding*).

ABOUT THE AUTHOR

Jon Del Arroz is a #1 Amazon Bestselling Steampunk author, "the leading Hispanic voice in science fiction" according to PJMedia.com, and winner of the 2018 CLFA Book of the Year Award for his novel, *For Steam And Country*. As a contributor to The Federalist, he is also recognized as a popular journalist and cultural commentator. Del Arroz writes science fiction, and comic books, and can be found most summer weekends in section 127 of the Oakland Coliseum cheering on the A's.

email: jdaguestposts (at) gmail (dot) com

ALSO BY JON DEL ARROZ

The Adventures Of Baron Von Monocle:

For Steam And Country

The Blood Of Giants

The Fight For Rislandia

The Iron Wedding

The Steam Knight

The Nano Templar Series

Justified

Sanctified

Glorified

The Aryshan War

The Stars Entwined

The Stars Asunder (2020)

Other Books

Make Science Fiction Fun Again

Star Realms: Rescue Run

Colony Launch (2020)

The Demon's Eye (2020)

Graphic Novels And Comics

Flying Sparks Volume 1

Flying Sparks Volume 2

Flying Sparks: Meta-Man Special

Flying Sparks Issue #0

The Ember War

www.ingramcontent.com/pod-product-compliance
Lightning Source LLC
Chambersburg PA
CBHW022136240626

47153CB00007B/2393